"I know

Ian tugged

his lap. Gently he eased her head onto his shoulder, then settled back into the couch.

"Is this all necessary?" she whispered.

"If we're going to do this, I want to be comfortable," he murmured, massaging the back of her neck.

The exhaustion crept up on her, taking advantage of her relaxing muscles. "We should be downstairs, tailing Novak," she grumbled halfheartedly.

"Not for a while. They'll become suspicious if we keep disappearing on them."

"Ian?" She yawned against his neck. "You never once asked me to prove the baby is yours."

"Because I know it's mine." Ian paused. "Because what happened between us wasn't ordinary, Red. It's our baby."

And come hell or Irish temper, he would protect his family.

DONNA YOUNG

THE BODYGUARD CONTRACT

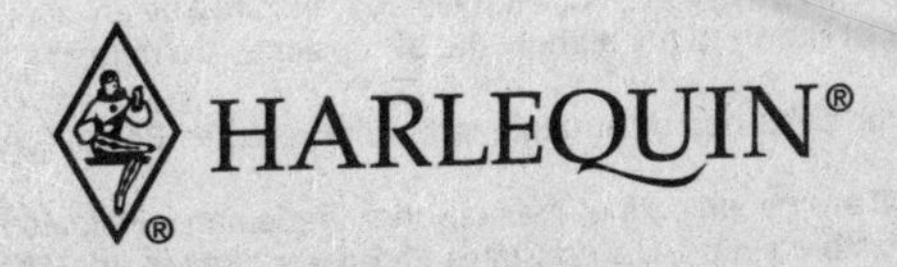

TORONTO • NEW YORK • LONDON
AMSTERDAM • PARIS • SYDNEY • HAMBURG
STOCKHOLM • ATHENS • TOKYO • MILAN • MADRID
PRAGUE • WARSAW • BUDAPEST • AUCKLAND

To Donald Prager, I love you, Dad

ISBN-13: 978-0-373-69234-7
ISBN-10: 0-373-69234-X

THE BODYGUARD CONTRACT

This edition published by arrangement with Harlequin Books S.A.

www.eHarlequin.com

Printed in U.S.A.

ABOUT THE AUTHOR

Donna Young, an incurable romantic, lives in beautiful Northern California with her husband and two children.

Books by Donna Young

HARLEQUIN INTRIGUE

824—BODYGUARD RESCUE
908—ENGAGING BODYGUARD
967—THE BODYGUARD CONTRACT

CAST OF CHARACTERS

Lara Mercer—A government operative determined to stop a biochemical weapon from destroying hundreds of Americans, whatever the price—until she realizes the price might be her child's life.

Ian MacAlister—An ex-Navy SEAL with a reputation for making the tough calls. But when a mission forces him to choose between saving the world and saving his family—can he walk away from love?

Father Xavier Varvarinski—A Russian double agent with a strong faith but a stronger desire to play God.

Anton Novak—An international arms dealer who controls a biochemical weapon powerful enough to wipe out an entire city—in addition to a government operative or two.

Chapter One

Electricity charged the air, preparing the night for the incoming storm. Black clouds swirled and thundered—a tempest in the midnight sky. From its center, spiraled a pair of sleek, nylon wings.

Lara Mercer ignored the storm and focused on her target—the crest of a concrete roof seventy stories above Central Park West. The wind burst beneath her, shoving her slightly off course. Immediately, she pulled the steering toggle, compensating.

One hundred feet…sixty…twenty. Another quick adjustment. After Lara's feet hit concrete, her thumb punched the small laser mechanism on her harness. The para wings fluttered, once…twice, then vanished into ash, allowing the brush of the wind to scatter the remains across the concrete and tar. While she had expected the result, her eyes widened in admiration. She crouched, gun in hand. Damn. Doctor Kate D'Amato was getting downright scary with her gadgets.

Lara checked the corners of the rooftop through infrared goggles. The light bounced against, then behind the walls and the air-conditioning units, telling her no one hid in wait.

The storm picked up, torrent gusts of air spitting rain and snow. Lara judged the distance between the Manhattan skyscrapers to be approximately fifty meters.

After moving to the three-foot concrete barrier surrounding the roof, she pointed her cable gun down and squeezed the eject trigger. The steel anchor shot into the cement floor with a loud, clipped *chink.* After testing the secure anchor, she hooked the loose end—a pulley—to her harness.

Quickly, she holstered her gun and jumped, feet-first. One…two. She eased the brake on the pulley, preventing the cable from jerking. Any movement against the windows triggered a vibration sensor imbedded in its tempered glass.

She braced her feet against the steel of the building, her knees relaxed. The targeting system on her infrared goggles locked on the building across the street—number two in the triad of buildings. Lara aimed the cable gun, pleased when the red stream of its laserscope cut through the falling snow.

Swiftly, she shot another cable, her lips tilting into a wicked grin when she saw she'd nailed her mark—six inches of steel separating twin panes of smoked glass.

Behind the window stood huge cooling units and

boilers. The rumble from the machinery made it impossible for the vibration sensors to function properly, so none had been installed. Mechanical floors were located every eighteen stories. This particular window was the closest to her objective—illegal arms dealing information on the hard drive of the corporate computer.

Glancing at her watch, she couldn't stop a rise of satisfaction. The mission, although difficult, had not proven impossible.

Suddenly, the whir of cable sliced through the wind. Within seconds, Lara's Glock was in her hand.

"Holster your weapon, Red." The voice rumbled low through the transmitter in her ear.

Lara pushed her goggles down, leaving them dangling around her neck. A figure, male, dressed in a black Lycra bodysuit identical to hers, slid into position beside her. Even with his face hooded, Lara recognized the wide shoulders, the lean waist and hips. She took a deep breath, resisted the flutter in her stomach.

"Damn it, Ian. You almost got yourself shot." Lara snapped the infrared specs back into place and shoved her pistol into her side holster.

"And here I thought you'd be glad to see me." Like Lara, Ian MacAlister braced himself against the building, feet spread.

"Get the hell out of here. This is my operation." Dismissing him, she linked her anchor cable to the one she'd just shot across to the second building. "I don't need you hovering like I'm some new trainee."

"You're acting like one. This is a level four mission," Ian said. His tone remained light, but his stance tightened. "Requires a minimum of two operatives."

"The *recommendation* is two operatives," she snapped, checking the lock on her harness, making sure it wouldn't move down the cable until she was ready. "It's not mandatory."

"Still trying to prove something to Daddy, Red?" Ian aimed his cable pistol and fired. She didn't have to look to know he'd placed the anchor close to hers.

Lara's back teeth slammed together. For the last few months, she'd dealt with Ian. Ever since he'd been attached to Labyrinth—an elite black ops division of the CIA.

At seventy stories, they both knew she wasn't in any position to stop him from joining her. And she wasn't about to scrub the mission.

Irritation gnawed at the base of her neck. The man looked harmless enough—a white muted figure through her infrared goggles—but experience had taught her that Ian MacAlister was dangerous. And more importantly, her heart had taught her that he wasn't to be trusted.

"I don't have to prove anything to anyone, Ian." It was no secret that Lara had to work harder than most Labyrinth operatives. Not because she was a woman, but because up until a few months ago, her father, Jonathon Mercer had been their boss. Now, he was the Vice President of the United States. "I don't need you to pull this off."

"Wanna bet?" Ian asked, hesitating, while he adjusted his own line, long enough to shoot her a sideways glance. "A small wager, just to make things interesting."

"No wager. No nothing. Just get the hell away from me." *Haven't you done enough?* Her mind screamed the question.

"What's the matter? Afraid?"

The taunt hit home, an arrow piercing the deepest part of her heart and feeding the rage at her own insecurities. Deftly, she attached a small portable winch to her cable and started tightening the gear. Within seconds, her line was taut. "First one in the building wins," she said, her voice flat, businesslike. But the air between them crackled and this time it wasn't the storm that created the electricity.

"Winner chooses the prize, Red?" His voice dipped into a slow, smoky burn that touched off a fire in her belly. Damn it. Only Ian MacAlister would consider seducing a woman dangling hundreds of feet above concrete.

"Yes," she accepted, knowing she'd left herself no other option. It had been months since he'd last worked with her. In that time her skills had sharpened, her strength grown.

A sudden rush of adrenaline shimmied up her spine. Ian was in for the surprise. Lara replayed the mission points in her head. Already, her little interaction with him had cost her time.

It took a few seconds for Ian to secure his line. In those moments, she'd thought about taking a head start, but it wasn't her way to cheat. She didn't want to give him any reason to cry foul when she won.

"Ready, sweetheart?"

Lara's nod was quick, decisive. "Go!"

Air blasted her face, hitting her with bits of ice and snow. Lara tuned it out along with the whine of Ian's cable beside her. Instead, she focused on her point of contact a few yards ahead.

Without warning, his cable jerked then dropped. He grabbed for his harness lock, catching the mechanism a split second before he dived into a sudden free fall.

The line snapped. An insidious crack exploded against the steel and glass. In the back of her mind, she registered the fact that she had yelled his name into their transmitter. He slammed against the window, took the impact with his shoulder, absorbing the punch with a grunt.

"Damn it, Ian," Lara bit out. "Hold on, I'm coming down."

"Stay there. I'm okay." A quick glance showed the end of his cable lashing through the air like a whip.

"My line broke loose from the winch. If I use my suction cups, I should be able to minimize any more vibrations."

"How hard did you hit the glass?"

"We'll find out, won't we?" They both knew he could've already set off the silent alarm. "Check the perimeter."

"I am." Lara tugged her mini computer out of her utility belt and scanned its screen. "So far we're secure," she advised, her tone flat but not convinced. "No hostile movement toward our position."

Ian grabbed the suction cups from his utility belt. A combination of rubber-rimmed steel and polyurethane, the suction cups locked over hands and knees allowing an individual to scale any smooth surface within minutes.

"Hurry up, Ian."

"I am—"

Ian dropped another floor. But this time when he grabbed for the rope, the suction cups fell to the street below. "Lara, my anchor slipped. I'm guessing my fall broke it free of the cement. It must have caught on the roof's railing. If I'm right, the anchor's not going to hold for long."

Lara swore. "Just hang tight. I'm repositioning myself, then I'm going to cut my cable."

"No! I'll climb my line. I think I can make it before—"

Time took the luxury of rapelling out of the

equation. Ignoring him, she unlocked her cinch and plunged into a free fall.

Seconds later, Ian dangled only a few feet away. "Take my hand!" she yelled.

He reached, grabbed. His anchor gave way. Lara braced her legs and absorbed the jerk of his fall.

"You okay?"

"Yes." She ignored the painful burn in her shoulder and reached for her knife. Quickly she cut him loose from the damaged cable.

His upper body flexed, then strained with the reach. He clipped his harness to her line. "I need to get above you for better traction. Slide onto my back."

She sheathed her knife. Using her free hand, she grabbed his shoulder and levered herself onto his back. Her fingers dug into his flesh, the firm muscles beneath soothing her fear.

In the distance, thunder rumbled and Lara froze recognizing the sound for what it was. "Chopper."

"Get in front of me, Red."

"No." She was literally covering his back, and from his tightened muscles against her chest, he wasn't pleased about it.

Ian swore. "That aerial's coming in fast. You can bet that any ammo it shoots will be armor piercing and kill us both, whether you're on my back or not. These bulletproof suits won't protect us one bit." Ian shifted, using one free hand to hike her higher on his hips. The *whop, whop* of a helicopter rose behind them. "On my shoulders! Now!"

Quickly, she hoisted herself up his back, knowing with each move, she left bruises. Sitting on his shoulders, she slid her harness up her rope, locked it in place above his harness, then braced her feet against the glass.

"Run!" Ian ordered before bumping her off her perch. Both sprinted using the rope tension to keep them perpendicular to the building.

Bullets strafed behind them, blowing out windows in their path.

"Jump!" he yelled.

The couple leaped in unison, the momentum creating a pendulum out of the rope, swinging them back behind the line of fire. Lara threw out one of her suction cups and anchored it above one of the blown-out windows.

Without words, he caught the edge of the sill. Muscles straining, he pulled himself up and in.

"He's coming around again," Lara shouted.

Ian hoisted her in next to him. She flopped, belly first to the floor.

Neither spoke. Shards of glass bit her hands. Ignoring it, she dived with Ian behind a huge oak desk. Bullets peppered the ground around them.

"Get ready." Lara palmed her gun and waited. Soon the helicopter hovered in front of the blown-out window.

Ian grabbed a miniature rocket from his utility belt, attached it to his cable pistol and fired. The whine of the missile pierced the air, hanging only a brief moment before it hit.

The helicopter exploded in a rush of flame and heat. Fireworks of metal and sparks rocketed through the room.

"So much for the silent approach," Ian yelled over the din, ignoring the spew of smoke already receding from the shattered window. "You okay?"

"Yes," Lara answered. Alarms sounded—huge foghorns that blasted through, shaking the floor beneath them.

She scanned the room, ignoring the howling gusts of wind from the missing windows. Like most executive offices, the decor was no more than sterile layers of chrome, leather and glass. Double doors in front. Single door at the side, just beyond a fully stocked bar. Probably to the private bathroom. She tugged off her goggles and pulled out a miniature, palm-sized computer again.

"How are we looking so far?" Ian asked, yanking off his own night goggles. The office was semidark but the hallways would be lit.

Lara glanced up from the green display. "We've got a minute max. I show six goons coming up the stairs. One in the elevator. Two more just outside the front doors."

In theory, they still had a mission to complete. The

question was, could they succeed and still save their skin? Ian gestured toward the entrance, indicating he'd take point. Lara covered.

Within seconds, two men burst through the double doors. Their Uzi semiautomatics strafed the room, ripping through paintings and leather upholstery. The bar's mirror exploded. Glass shards sprayed across their heads.

Lara dropped, rolled, came up on her knees, catching the farthest gunman off guard. When he swung back, she fired. But she'd misjudged the quickness of his reflexes. Pain exploded in her stomach, the impact knocking her back. She gasped as white-hot fire spiked her from belly to chest.

Ian jerked when she fell but didn't turn until the two men dropped, dead, on the ground. Quickly, he grabbed their guns. "How bad?"

She clutched her stomach, covering the bullet wound. Fear rose, coating her tongue with acid and bile. "It's nothing." She moved, using the desk to stand. Lara fought off the wave of nausea and weakness. "Let's finish this," she whispered. Blood soaked her suit. She could feel the warm stickiness against her skin. She shifted her weapon to her left hand and braced her legs apart to keep them from shaking. "Options?"

"Stairs." Ian snagged her computer and glanced at the screen. "I've got four more closing in."

Lara nodded, only to stop when the room tilted.

The loss of blood was already making her light-headed. "Let's go."

She staggered a few steps, then recovered long enough to reach the wall next to the double doors. Light from the hallway spewed into the office, its glare almost painful to Lara's blurring vision. Taking short shallow breaths, she waited for Ian to give the go-ahead.

"Get ready, Red."

"I'm ready." She gripped the weapon tight to cover her trembling. With a jerk, she slid closer to the door.

Ian glanced back at her and swore.

Lara followed his gaze. Blood streaked the wall behind her.

The bullet had gone completely through and out her back.

Angry with herself for not realizing, she said, "There's nothing you can do, Ian, except get us the hell out of here."

Lara wasn't a woman who relinquished control. She'd learned long ago that doing so would only bring pain. This time, ironically, pain was forcing her to do just that, leaving her no choice but to trust Ian to save them. "You've got about five minutes, hotshot. Then you're going to have to carry me."

"When this is over..." Gun raised, Ian used his foot to kick the double door open. The ding of the elevator ricocheted through the white hallway. "Get down!" he ordered, then grabbed a compact explosive, the size of a small metal hockey puck, from his belt. He tossed it directly into the path of the elevator and shoved Lara into a nearby doorway, shielding her body with his.

The explosion rocked the floor. A burst of heat surrounded them, rancid smoke of burned tile and plaster filled her lungs. Lara coughed, tasting the blood and bile.

Ian eased back, his eyes finding hers. “Can you make it?”

“I’m tougher than I look,” she whispered through the viselike pain that squeezed her chest, then prayed she was right.

Without help, Lara reached the stairway door first, but it was Ian who yanked it open.

Somewhere below the slap of running shoes echoed through the circular concrete stairway. Ian motioned her up the stairs.

Her legs grew weaker, shaking uncontrollably. She grabbed the railing to pull herself up the steps, but her hands, slick with sweat, slid. With a cry, she fell facefirst onto the concrete. Pain exploded in her chest, seared her belly.

“Lara.”

“Go,” she rasped. Blood bubbled up her throat, making each breath an effort.

Ian grabbed her by the shoulder, his arms braced to lift her.

“No!” The fire in her gut intensified. Weakly, she

lifted her hand, showing him the steel puck clutched under her fingers. "Get out of here."

Before she set the timer, Ian's hand covered hers.

Too weak to tug free, she didn't even try. "Let go, Ian. I'll detonate it when they reach me. By the time their friends realize you're not here, you'll have the files and be long gone."

"No." He swung her up into his arms, pausing when she gasped with pain. "Not this time."

A man yelled from the stairs. Lara heard the blast of gunfire, felt Ian shudder with each bullet's impact. The warmth of his blood mingled with hers, its metallic scent suspended between them.

Slowly he pressed her back against the wall, his body now more deadweight than not. Still, he protected her.

"Ian," she rasped, ignoring the movement behind them, the growing echo of feet as the bad guys closed in. Instead, she concentrated on the small flecks of silver in his blue irises, the rapid beat of his heart beneath her fingertips—trying to absorb the strength behind each. "Game over."

"No, Red, it's just beginning." Ian leaned in until his lips hovered only slightly above hers, his breath brushed warm, reassuring against her cheek. Anticipation—and maybe a little panic—rifled through her and came out in a shuddered breath. All she needed to do was lift her chin….

"I breached the building first."

Chapter Two

"Damn it, MacAlister!" Lara sat up, pulled her hands out of the computer cuffs and tugged off her Virtual Imaging helmet. A cascade of red hair tumbled free. With fast, jerky movements, she disconnected the sensor wires from her training suit. An instant later, lights flashed on and the VI program shut down—leaving all four walls of the lab room an iridescent blue and the air silent. Anger whipped through her. "You sabotaged my operation, didn't you?"

Ian removed his helmet, tossed it into the leather seat next to him. He ran a casual hand through his chestnut hair, now sweat darkened to a charred brown. Cropped military short, his hairstyle complemented the broad sweep of his cheekbones, the hard line of his jaw and a nose that was a touch off center and, she suspected, had been broken more than once.

"Answer me, MacAlister," she demanded. Born

from a French mother and an Irish father, Lara had more than her fair share of temper. Most times, she kept a tight rein of control over it. Other times…

"I can't. I'm dead, remember?"

"Funny," she bit out the word. "Did you or did you not sabotage my operation?"

"Now why would I do that?" His mouth twitched with amusement. "I'm the one who developed the program."

No one would call Ian MacAlister handsome in a pretty boy sense. But with the strong, striking features of his Celtic ancestors and his laser-blue eyes, no woman could walk past him without a second glance.

"Who better to change it?" she snapped, finding her own eyes lingering, her heartbeat accelerating. Annoyed, she shoved her hair behind her ear and slid from the leather seat.

"All the programs have failure sequences in them," he responded with equanimity. He disconnected his suit and stood in one long, fluid movement—a jungle cat satisfied after a night on the prowl. "No mission goes smoothly."

"Usually, it's a random process," she argued, cursing herself for letting her guard down. "This time you decided what was going to happen and when. That's why you made the bet with me. Isn't it?"

"You decided the challenge, not me. Besides, I didn't need to reprogram anything to win. The fact that you went in by yourself told me you hadn't thought the mission through." He slid the zipper on his training suit down to his waist. He wore no shirt. Lara's gaze flickered over him, settling on the ripple of movement across his chest as he jerked his arms free. He left the top portion of the suit dangling off his hips.

Her eyes dipped, following each carved muscle that flexed with power under his sun-bronzed skin—remembering from months before how the bare skin gave way to a small, sexy line of sable hair just below his navel. Too damn sexy for her own good, she understood now. Still, the heat danced through her, lighting little fires along her nerves.

His gaze caught hers, and in an instant the planes of his face sharpened, his jaw tightened with awareness.

With effort, she drew one deep steadying breath.

Then just that quick Ian's features smoothed, the passion sliding under a relaxed, easy smile—an undeniable arrogance.

He turned to retrieve a white towel from the console beside his chair and Lara let out a long hiss.

Ian glanced over his shoulder in understanding. "How's the damage?"

Welts, raised and vivid, striped his back. "Not too bad for a tough guy like you." Lara waved a careless hand, not pleased with the chaotic emotions that squeezed her chest like an accordion.

"You had the sensors set too high."

"I wanted the pain to be realistic," she stated. "We both know the results are only superficial. Harmless."

For the first time she noticed the burning across her abdomen. After placing her helmet on a nearby console, Lara unzipped her suit and stepped out of it, revealing her white sport bra and fitted racing briefs that rode low on her hips. Above her waistband were dozens of welts, the intensity already fading into dull red splotches. Lara resisted the urge to soothe the sting and her stomach beneath.

"You've only yourself to blame if you're sore, Ian." Lara's gaze cut back. "You should have left me to take care of the bad guys. I was dead anyway."

"I don't leave anyone behind."

"That's right, I forgot," Lara said, knowing that Ian had resigned his naval commission only months before contracting his talents to Labyrinth. "It's the Navy SEAL way. So is integrity. Honor." She inclined her head, letting him see that she remembered the day he'd held no such honor. "Huah." Her blatant sarcasm couldn't be missed when she uttered the Navy SEALs' signature expression.

"It's my way," he answered, this time all traces of humor gone.

"Just stay out of *my* way," Lara insisted, noting his deepened displeasure and not caring. Caring would show that he meant something to her. Had the means to hurt her again.

The fury was there, rigid but contained. She

tossed her suit over the back of the chair and started toward the double steel doors. "And stay out of my training sessions. I don't need a partner. And if I did, it wouldn't be you."

Ian's frown deepened, his eyes slanted into blue slits—sharp enough to slice the air between them. "Wanna bet?"

Slowly, she swung around, her own eyes narrowing. And because her temper broke free, she snarled. "Are you *trying* to piss me off?"

"Face it, Red, just the fact that right now I'm sharing the same air pretty much puts you into tilt." He rubbed the towel over his face, now seemingly indifferent to her fury.

"I'm done with the games, Ian." She didn't argue with his first statement. The truth was the truth.

"So am I." Cain MacAlister, the new director of Labyrinth and Ian's older brother, stepped into the blue room. His gaze slid to Lara. "Don't you have a plane to catch?"

"I have time," Lara answered. Both brothers moved with predatory ease, but whether it was because of their warrior heritage or occupations, Lara couldn't be sure—the ability seemed so innate. Where Ian was muscle and meat, Cain was leaner, almost lanky, with pitch-black hair, smoky gray eyes and features sharp enough to be called aristocratic.

Still their jawlines were the same, Lara noted.

And Lord knew, so was the slant of their frowns.

Cain glanced from Lara to Ian. "Are you two done playing?"

"We're done all right," Lara answered easily.

But Ian saw the proud line of her jaw lift. Lara didn't like Cain's question, but Ian knew she wouldn't address the issue with Cain in Ian's presence. Too bad, he decided, because he would have really liked to see her take on his brother.

"For now," Ian commented, while his gaze remained on Lara, unblinking. He rested a hip on the nearby console. "It was Lara's doing," he said, deliberately taunting the Irish in her. "The woman can't leave me alone," he added, pleased when temper whipped color into the delicate line of her cheeks and her eyes sharpened into jaded glass. And a little disappointed, he mused, when stubbornness had her biting back words that threatened to get past the generous curve of her mouth.

"Ian." Those same lips thinned over her teeth into a vicious smile. "Drop dead."

She slapped her hand against the door panel, then paused long enough to wait for the door to slide open.

"Lara," Cain called. "Stop by Kate's office. She has a few…devices…that might come in handy for your meeting."

Kate D'Amato was Ian's younger sister and the head of Labyrinth's technology division. "I will." With one nod, Lara left.

Cain shook his head after the door slid shut. "A little early in the morning for a taste of sadomasochism, isn't it?"

Ian sheathed the razor-sharp need that swiped at his gut. Some would describe Lara as slender, willowy—the more romantic, maybe—with long, tangled curls of fire-red hair and eyes the color of the Emerald City itself.

But Lara was far from romantic. Her body, kept lean and strong from a stringent physical regime, was no more than another weapon to use when necessary.

"Beats a strong cup of coffee," Ian growled, and because it was only his brother, letting his frustration show. "God save me from stubborn women. She deliberately set herself up to fail. It's as if she has to keep proving to herself she's competent. You and I both know she's one of the best operatives here."

"Funny thing is, we both might know it, but you continually come to her rescue." Cain folded his arms. The sleek, tailored lines of his navy-blue suit emphasized the air of authority.

Something, Ian thought perversely, Cain was very much aware of and used to his advantage. "Up to today, I've done a damn good job avoiding her. Then I get your message ordering me here at 0600 hours."

"You work for me. I can do that," Cain reminded Ian.

"Still, you don't have to get so much pleasure from it."

"True," Cain agreed before his tone grew serious.

"Ian, if you need to talk, I'm all ears. Remember what I went through with Celeste?"

Ian smiled at the mention of his new sister-in-law, Celeste Pavenic-MacAlister. A tiny bit of a woman, she was the best damn profiler Labyrinth had.

A few months back she'd led Cain on a merry chase. She'd changed her identity and went into hiding to stop the President's assassination. "You're in love with Celeste. Big difference."

Cain being in love was still a new concept for Ian. While Cain was the cool, collected one, their sister, Kate, was logical to a fault. As the middle sibling, Ian was the emotional one—quick to laugh, quicker to temper.

A challenging balance of personalities, their mother always said. But one that seemed to work. Because of this, Cain had been Ian's sounding board since they were children. But for some reason, his problem with Lara was too intimate to even share with his brother. "I can handle it." To take the bite out of his answer, Ian added, "But I appreciate the concern...and the offer. Enough to take a rain check."

"You won't have time for a rain check, not for the next few days anyway. You're going on assignment. I need you to keep track of an operative."

"Anyone I know?" Ian asked before rubbing the towel over his head. Hell, tracking had long been Ian's specialty, so the request didn't surprise him. It would do him good, too, to take his mind off—

"Lara."

Ian stopped midstroke, his eyes hardened. "No."

"It's not a suggestion, Ian, it's an order. You're under contract. Remember?"

"Only for a few more months."

"Well, it's a good thing that watching Lara's back should only take the rest of today," Cain drawled.

"Is she in danger?"

"No," Cain answered, but the word rang with caution. "Not at the moment. But my little voice is working overtime on the possibility."

Over the years, Cain, like Kate and Ian, had learned to accept the inner warnings, to trust them. A gift from their ancestors, their father said, passed down through strong Scots blood.

"So in other words, you need a babysitter." Ian used the agency's slang for bodyguard with derision. "I've been there, done that. No thank you." He turned his back on Cain, using the few seconds of reprieve to push back a wave of concern. "Have Quamar do it. She *likes* him. And it's just the right type of mission to get him back in the groove again." An ex-Mossad agent, Quamar Bazan was one of the few Labyrinth operatives the MacAlister brothers would trust protecting their loved ones.

"Quamar might have his eyesight back, but he hasn't been cleared by the doctors for duty." A few months prior, their friend had taken a gunshot to the head while protecting the President's mother. It was a miracle he had survived. “You’re the only one I can send at this point.”

“Why?”

“You’re going to ask me that after what I just saw?” Cain glanced at the Virtual Imaging equipment.

“What you just saw was none of your business,” Ian bit out. “Pull her from the mission or assign someone else.”

“She’s neck deep in it. Pulling her now would blow months of work.”

Lara had joined Labyrinth three years prior. Ever since, she’d been neck deep in one situation or another. “Lara’s at the top of her game when the pressure’s on.”

“But this time I’m not confident her mind is in the game.”

“We are talking about Lara Mercer? All business, no personality?” The words tumbled out like dry, bitter leaves. Ian rubbed his face with both hands, ignoring the whiskers that scraped his palm. God, he was tired. Of the espionage, the endless chasing after bad guys—dealing with his feelings for Lara. “Forget I said that.”

“Ian, you’re the logical choice.”

“Trust me, Cain, there’s nothing logical about Lara and I. You don’t want to send me.” Ian reached for his gym bag to snag a cigarette, then swore. He’d quit months before, but the craving still gnawed at him.

“You’re right, I don’t.”

Ian stared at his brother for a moment. It wasn't in Cain's nature to jump into decisions. If anything, he was too cautious. Most times, Cain made sure he'd always had a backup plan on any mission.

Obviously, Ian was that backup plan. "All right, boss," he said, resigned. "Fill me in."

Cain walked over to a nearby computer console and hit a few buttons. "Later today, Lara's meeting with this man."

A picture flashed against the back wall. A priest, posed in a professional portrait. An older man with strands of hair smoothed over a slightly shiny head. A hint of a smile added mischief to an otherwise plain face. "Father Xavier Varvarinski. Retired. St. Stanislaus Roman Catholic Church, Las Vegas."

"I'm listening," Ian growled. Only Lara could be at risk dealing with a priest.

"Father Xavier," Cain repeated, "is Russian intelligence. A double agent for Labyrinth operations. Been in the business longer than you and I put together," he explained. "As a priest, he's had access to most of the Russian terrorist leaders and Russian Mafia members." His gaze shifted to Ian. "I've never dealt with him directly, but he's good. Very good."

Ian studied the picture, noted the worn creases, the laugh lines. Evidence the priest spent most of his time enjoying life. But the weariness that dulled the blue of the man's eyes caused a jab of trepidation deep in Ian's belly. "When was this picture taken?"

"Six months ago."

A lot can happen in six months. "Is he a real priest?" Ian wondered aloud. They'd all used different aliases at one time or another. Impersonating a priest was no different than pretending to be a cop, or a doctor.

"Yes. Served in Vietnam in his early thirties. Studied for the priesthood after his discharge. Seems he got his calling somewhere in the midst of that mess."

"Interesting way to combine two careers," Ian commented, then hung his towel loosely around the back of his neck. Only his white-knuckle grip on each end gave away his edginess. "I assume this priest has information regarding the biochemical."

"Actually, it's in his possession...." Cain paused. "*It* being Substance 39."

Ian let out a slow whistle. "So the rumors are true then. We have a new biochemical warfare weapon to worry about."

"While the Russians have tagged it with their usual substance number, on the streets it's called *Katts Smeart*. The English translation...Silent Death."

Cain moved on to the next slide. This time it was a newspaper photo of a man behind a podium—average height, slight in build, with properly trimmed brown hair, peppered with gray. His style was just short of slick. Not too Hollywood. But close.

"*Katts Smeart* is a synthetically enhanced poison allegedly financed and created by this man, Mikhail

Davidenko, leader of the Russian terrorist sect—The Maxim. A fact the Russian government has conveniently overlooked. And the Russian Mafia has embraced."

"Davidenko." Ian recalled the name, acknowledging the punch of caution that jarred his spine. "Involved mostly with gambling, drug and human trafficking, arms and nuclear material dealings—even the sale of body organs. I'm not surprised about the biochemical warfare. Only that it took him so long."

The next picture appeared on the wall—an aerial view of Davidenko on his yacht, entertaining. "Bottom line with Davidenko is profit. Biochemical manufacturing is big business these days," Cain said.

Ian noted a few politicians, European and American—all dressed designer casual and surrounded by topless, thong-clad beauties. "Amazing what dirty money can buy."

Cain grunted in agreement.

Ian considered the photograph again. "And Lara?"

"She's been tracking Davidenko, gathering information through Father Xavier. We've always suspected Davidenko's involvement in illegal activities within our borders. But never had proof."

"The Maxim has a pretty long reach." Lara's involvement didn't surprise him. The woman could find trouble going to the Laundromat. "How in the hell did the priest get a hold of the poison in the first place?"

Cain flashed another picture. This one was a woman. A brunette with classical features that complemented her upswept hair, wearing a strapless, black Versace gown.

In this photo, Davidenko stood to her right whispering in her ear. The curve of her mouth showed her amusement, but it was the softness in the deep brown eyes that confirmed much more.

"She's amused, but not in love," Ian murmured, his opinion instinctive.

"Her name is Sophia Franco," Cain continued. But the slight raise of his brow acknowledged Ian's comment.

"The actress?" Ian remembered Sophia Franco. Late thirties. Never headlined. Her forte was horror movies. Got a lot of press over her blood-chilling screams.

"Davidenko's mistress," Cain stated. "A few months back, Father Xavier managed an introduction. She's a Roman Catholic and has become quite attached to the old man."

"Are you saying Sophia Franco managed to get the poison to the priest?"

"It fits," Cain responded. "We have proof that Father Xavier controls her. It's no secret Russian terrorism is a small step from the Russian Mafia."

"So, Sophia Franco turns in the *Katts Smeart* hoping to save lives and her soul? Hell of a penance." Ian frowned. "Where is she?"

"Dead, we suspect. But I haven't been able to confirm it yet," Cain said, then paused. "Lara's the courier for the *Katts Smeart.* She's headed for Las Vegas where Father Xavier is supposed to pass it to her later today."

"So Lara gets the weapon, brings it in," Ian said, relaxing somewhat. "One-two punch. She could handle this in her sleep. If you send me in to cover her and she finds out—it won't be pretty."

"Pretty is the least of my worries. After this assignment, I'm forcing Lara to take a leave of absence. For her benefit." Another pause, this time longer. "And yours."

"Mine? How in the hell do you figure that?" He followed Cain's gaze to the VI equipment. "You're not getting rid of her because the two of us can't get along, are you? Because if that's the case, I'll step down. Lara's hated my guts ever since the President fiasco two months ago." And rightly so, Ian silently acknowledged. "If she loses her career because of me, you're signing my death warrant."

"A few days ago, I would've agreed with you," Cain reasoned. "But now, circumstances have changed. If her mission goes wrong and you have to intervene…" Cain rubbed the back of his neck. "Well, let's just say I'm betting she'll accept your help. Past or no past."

"And why is that?"

"Because whether I like it or not, in the last

twenty-four hours this mission became personal," Cain responded, the hard edge back in his tone. "Lara fainted during a workout here at the center. I ordered her to get a physical. At the time, our doctors suspected anemia and took some blood samples."

"And?" Ian stiffened, not bothering to cover the thread of concern. To his knowledge, Lara had never been sick a day in her life. "Was it?"

"No," Cain admitted slowly, studying his brother. "She's two months pregnant."

Chapter Three

Las Vegas, Nevada. Wednesday, 1400 hours

Father Xavier Varvarinski slipped off his wire-rimmed glasses, placed them beside the Bible cradled in his lap, then eased back against his hard, pine chair. Instantly, a rush of relief flooded the ache between his shoulder blades.

Even so, Xavier held his sigh of pleasure in check, not wanting the soft sound to rupture the peace that surrounded him. It wasn't the heavy silence of the faithful which dominated most Sunday masses. Instead, it was a comforting silence—a reassuring murmur so fluid, it slid easily past the miniscule gaps in the confessional's aged maple walls.

With his joints aching from arthritis and his lungs frail from years of tobacco abuse, Xavier had little that comforted him physically.

A true sign of being old he supposed. Still, he found solace in the midweek confessions and had insisted on upholding St. Stanislaus's tradition when the current, younger pastor would've forgone the routine.

The hinges of the confessional door creaked, interrupting his thoughts. The priest's lips lifted into a small empathetic smile. There was nothing wrong with finding reassurance in the familiar.

After a few seconds, cloth rustled against the wooden kneeler, forcing Xavier to shift forward in his chair and put his glasses back on. Reverently, his palm slid over his Bible's leather cover—his finger-tips automatically settling into its aged creases. Another comfort. The most important.

"Good afternoon, Father." The hushed feminine greeting penetrated the screen.

"Eos," Xavier said, turning toward the familiar voice, wincing slightly at the sharp jab of pain deep in his chest.

The ceiling light cast a slim, feminine shadow against the confessional screen. The woman was young, not more than thirty, he assumed. Her tem-perament soft, serene.

Xavier reached in his pocket and withdrew his pills. "Once again, your promptness astounds me," he answered in Russian, then swallowed two tablets, dry.

"I received your message this morning." Her tone remained hushed, her dialect now Russian, also. "Do you have the package?"

"Yes," Xavier responded quietly. "You've told no one?"

"No one," Lara replied, the lie sliding easily off her tongue. "But time is not our friend right now, Father. I need that package."

"First things first, my child."

Lara's lips tilted into a half smile, forgetting for a moment the priest inside the man. "Of course."

Xavier made the sign of the cross. "In the name of the Father, and the Son and the Holy Spirit."

"Amen," Lara answered.

"May God keep you safe in his kingdom, Eos."

"Thank you. And you, also," she responded automatically, somewhat taken aback by the gesture. "Something is wrong." She noticed it in his tone—an underlying despair that Lara had heard many times during her career as a government operative. "What is it?"

He sighed. "I had prayed that this day wouldn't come, but it seems God's will is stronger than my pleas."

"What do you mean? Have you been discovered? Are you in danger?"

"Danger? No," Xavier responded slowly, as if searching for the right words. "I'm too old, and no longer a threat to anyone."

"Then why pray for—"

"Did you know that the true test of faith is when God doesn't answer our prayers? Most always he has a higher purpose. One that may eventually come to light. Still it is hard for me to believe that he would not prevent this. No matter his purpose."

"Surely, our purpose is the same, Father. To protect the innocent. You've done the government a huge favor by confiscating the substance. If there is anything I can do—"

"That's exactly why I sent for *you,* Eos. I need help in saving a great deal of lives." The priest hesitated, the uncertainty palpable. "I want to give you something. It's under your kneeler."

With deliberate movements, Lara reached under, her fingertips instantly touching small round beads. Slowly, she picked up the rosary. It was beautiful and old. "Is it yours?" A string of freshwater pearls looped a simple silver cross—on it, the image of Jesus suffering. The stark lines, the agonized expression were vivid in the dim light of the confessional.

"Yes. I've had it for many years."

"It's beautiful," Lara murmured. She grasped the cross in her fingers, surprised over the chill of the metal against her skin. Somehow she'd expected it to be warm. "I can't take this."

"You must. It is the key to my situation."

"I don't understand." Lara frowned, turning the cross over in her hand.

"You will."

"Father, I don't have time for cryptic puzzles. Tell me what you need."

"I need you to bring Anton Novak to me."

"The arms dealer?" She let out a low laugh. "I realize what you've provided to our government is beyond our expectations. But Novak?" She shook her head. "That's impossible. He's Mikhail Davidenko's right-hand man." Lara's fingers tightened on the rosary. "Why?"

"It doesn't matter. What matters is that I must see him within the next forty-eight hours." He slid an envelope through a thin gap at the bottom of the screen. "He is meeting a client here. At midnight tonight."

Lara glanced down at the information, saw an electronic key card with it. "And the key?"

"The key is to a room at the Château Bontecou. Room seven twenty one. I'm registered under the name Jim Brisbane. Bring Novak there and wait for me."

"Father, maybe if you tell me what you're involved in—"

"It's personal, little one. Very personal."

"A vendetta?"

"More like a contract," he admitted. "With God."

Trepidation slithered, coating her spine like slick oil. "I will keep your secrets. I always have. I promise. You have only to tell me—"

"I've told you what I need. And you can keep your promise by doing what I ask." Impatience deepened his accent.

With his impatience, came hers. "I'm sorry, Father, even if I could figure a way, I would need a reason. And my superiors' approval. Even then, I would require more than forty-eight hours. Anton Novak is a dangerous man."

"Dangerous is a relative term," he whispered. "Look, Eos, I have the biochemical your government wants. Enough to wipe out an entire city."

Everything in Lara stilled. "And I told you, we are very grateful."

"Then understand, I wouldn't put you in this position except you're my last hope. Bring me Novak. And tell no one."

"Or?"

"Or I will be forced to release the poison on thousands of people."

"I don't believe you," she whispered, her words urgent. "We've known each other too long. You would not kill innocents."

"It's in your best interest to believe me. What's at stake is worth far more than my immortal soul." She heard the scrape of his chair, the grunt of effort it took him to stand. "You are my only option. And I'm sorry for it. Now that you've accepted my gift, you have no choice."

His gift? Lara gripped the silver tight, understanding. "You poisoned the cross." Her stomach pitched, then rolled. "How long do I have?"

"Long enough." Behind the determination, she heard the sympathy. "Once you have Anton Novak in your custody, take him to Las Vegas. Wait at the Château Bontecou and I will contact you within the next twenty-four hours. You give me Anton Novak and I will give you *Katts Smeart* and its antidote."

"There's an antidote." Lara shuddered with relief.

"Yes, there is." Xavier sighed, as if his burden suddenly seemed too much. "I'm sorry, little one, but I couldn't take the chance that you would not help me. Work quickly, any longer than forty-eight hours and the antidote will not save you." He hesitated for a moment. "Please. No innocents need be involved. Not if you handle this problem for me."

After raising his hand, he once again made the sign of the cross. "God be with you, my child." With that, Father Xavier Varvarinski stepped out of the confessional.

Lara listened to the receding footsteps, understanding that it would be of no use to follow him. Not even to tell him he was wrong. Her uncontaminated hand slid to her stomach. Innocents were already involved.

Mojave Desert, North of Las Vegas
Wednesday, 2200 hours

PREGNANT. For the hundredth time, she pressed her fingers to her lids and swore. She'd never been one to cry before—not because of any sort of toughness or principle, but simply because she wasn't capable—could never find the release mechanism within her.

Now she didn't have eyes, she thought with

disgust, she had two spigots. Both spurting water at the slightest emotional whim.

Lara glanced up at the stars, their shine all flash and sass against the shaded layers of the indigo sky. It seemed pregnancy, or more specifically her whacked-out hormones, had found that mechanism.

With a sigh, she turned toward the north, searching the sky, using the diversion to undermine the chaotic emotions churning within.

She saw the belt first, its stars winking—bright beacons that led her to the sword. Within moments, she'd outlined the whole constellation. Orion.

Jerk.

If only she hadn't let her guard down, hadn't allowed herself to find solace in his arms. Humiliation rose to her throat, but anger caused the muscles to constrict. If only…

Damn Ian. It wasn't supposed to happen this way. She'd been taking the shots of progesterone for birth control and never had a problem—until now.

She'd been close to her goals. Goals she'd set long ago. Ones that didn't include children or marriage.

Mercers weren't meant for relationships, or families. So where did that leave her? "Getting through the next three days," she promised, determined. Then what?

She concentrated on her surroundings. An ocean of sand stretched between her and the horizon—with nothing between except boulders, scrub bushes… and the occasional tumbleweeds the wind tossed about.

In the distance, a diesel engine rumbled and gravel crunched, shattering the desert's tranquility. She crouched behind the boulder, peered through her infrared binoculars until she caught the shimmer of movement. Soon a semi appeared, its black cab blending easily in the darkness. The steel of its tractor trailer flashed—a mirror reflecting the moonlight. Lara's thumb pushed the zoom on her binoculars for a closer look.

Flanking one side was a dark sedan. Automatically, Lara noted the license plate.

When both the big rig and car slowed down to a snails pace, she glanced at her wristwatch.

Half an hour early. How convenient.

Within minutes, the two vehicles stopped, but their headlights remained on, the engines running.

The driver of the diesel immediately jumped out of the cab, his potbelly heaving with the effort. With urgent, bowlegged strides he headed for the nearest bush.

Long trip, Lara mused. She kept the driver in her peripheral vision, heard his grunt of relief, while she scanned the perimeter.

The semi's headlights glared through the sedan's back window revealing two men. Almost immediately, the driver of the sedan got out. Dressed in a leather jacket and jeans, the guy resembled a walking bald, brick wall with enough bulked-up muscle to make her wonder if he'd been nursed on steroids.

Once, just once, she'd like to see a hired thug with limbs the size of twigs.

Steroid Boy chose to stay near the car. His eyes expertly took in the immediate area. In one hand, he held a deadly Uzi. Keeping beat to some unknown tune, he tapped the weapon against his thigh.

The other driver had finished his business. He returned to his perch in the big rig's cab, then lit a cigarette.

Lara sat on the ground, her back against the boulder and considered her next move. Three men. Less than she expected from Novak.

After checking her utility belt, she twisted the silencer onto her Glock and glanced once more over the top of the boulder. Assured no one had moved, she slid her ski mask into place and took a deep breath.

Using the shadows for cover, she maneuvered through the sparse cover of boulders and brush until she reached the back of the semi's trailer. Easily thirteen feet in length, it could carry millions of dollars worth of illegal arms.

A cough echoed in the night air. Harmless. Still, she waited a scant few seconds before tugging the swing doors' lever. Locked. Not surprised, she tucked her gun into her waistband, grabbed the hinge and boosted herself onto the bumper.

The top of the trailer was a good four feet above

her own five-seven height. She took a deep breath and jumped. Her fingertips snagged the edge of the steel roof and she shimmied up to the top of the trailer.

Flat against the top, Lara's quick scan told her no one had moved. She tugged a rope free from her belt—a long cable of solid, moldable acid. Quickly, she placed it in a tight circle on the steel roof then reached for a small plastic bottle with the activating solution. She attached a climbing suction cup in the middle and poured the solution over the rope.

Soon acid ate through steel. The smell, only slightly pungent, lost its fierceness in the desert wind.

With a quick tug on the suction cup, Lara broke the steel free.

A chopper sounded in the distance and Lara swore. Hastily, she slid down the side panel of the truck, then hung by her fingers on its edge and waited.

The helicopter landed a hundred feet from the front of the diesel engine. The blades kicked up sand and debris, forcing Lara to turn away.

Using her arms, she pulled herself back to the top, wincing when steel scraped against her belly.

The copter's blades slowed. Two men jumped to the ground, both in suits, one carrying a briefcase—a large enough case to hold quite a bit of cash—while a younger man with black hair and a beard carried a machine gun. The pilot, she noticed, stayed in the helicopter.

A man, in his midthirties, stepped out from the

sedan. With a cigarette hanging from thin lips and sporting short, blond tipped hair—spiked like a David Bowie wannabe—the man waved a casual hand in greeting. Novak.

Shifting for a better view, she slowly drew her miniature binoculars, trying to get a read on the faces, the movement of their lips. Her frown deepened. Nothing.

Suddenly, Novak slapped the buyer on the shoulder and nodded toward the big rig driver.

The trailer door banged, sending a shock wave rippling through the steel beneath her. Lara pulled out her silencer pistol.

She listened, heard the laughter, recognized the underlying tone of satisfaction. Novak and his buyer climbed into the trailer, leaving the two bodyguards outside.

Lara scowled, but didn't waste time on the slight glitch. She grabbed the gas canister from her utility belt, pulled the release and dropped the cylinder through.

Swiftly, she covered the hole. Shouts of alarm penetrated the trailer walls. The Uzi guys came running, each taking a side. Lara aimed, fired, taking down the buyer's man with a bullet in the throat. With a cry of pain, he grasped his neck, the blood already gurgling between his gasps of breath. Lara ignored him, knowing the man was already dead.

Steroid Boy was much smarter. He dropped, rolled, then came to his knees and fired.

A rapid spray of bullets hit the air, pinging the steel beneath her. Lara twisted, grabbed the trailer's opposite edge and dropped. She scrambled under the rig. Exhaust and the scent of gasoline thickened the air beneath. Nausea roped through her belly. Ignoring it, she aimed at the booted feet and squeezed the trigger. An agonized scream tore through the air. The man dropped, both ankles shattered by bullets. One more to the chest took him out of the picture.

The copter pilot fired its machine gun. Bullets kicked up the dirt between the car and trailer, catching the semi's driver in their path. He jerked once, then fell to his knees. With eyes frozen open, he landed facefirst on the ground.

"Nice aim, idiot," Lara murmured, then rolled back into the open air and fired. The helicopter's windshield exploded and on its heels came another agonizing scream of pain.

Lara dropped her clip and shoved in her spare. Using the tires for cover, she waited two slow minutes. Bit by bit she crept around the back, knowing one or more of the men could've made it out before the gas rendered them unconscious.

She levered herself up, checked the darkness for signs of movement, then maneuvered around the stacked crates.

Both Novak and his buyer lay slumped on the floor—the briefcase at their feet.

Lara grabbed the case and straightened. Almost instantly, a bullet punched her chest. She flew back, her shoulder slammed against the wall of the rig.

Pain exploded from chest to chin. It knocked her legs out from under her. One of the men tackled her, sending them both out of the trailer and onto the dirt.

Before she could stop him, Novak reared back and whipped off her mask.

"Well, look what we've got here."

"Surprise." She rammed her knee into his crotch. Novak went down gasping. Lara jumped up, grabbed his hair and yanked his head back. Placing the gun just under his jaw.

"Okay, Tony. I don't have time for any guessing games. So for each correct answer you get to stay healthy. Each wrong answer, you get a bullet in a vital organ. Got me?"

"You *realize* who I am?" His eyes narrowed, but she noticed he still gasped out the words and took a great deal of pleasure in it.

"Well, after you get done being my bargaining chip, I'll ask you for an autograph. How's that?"

"Bargaining chip?"

"Later." Lara took a quick glance around. "How many of your guys are watching from the sidelines?"

"None," he denied, his tone artificially friendly. "Armand and I have been doing business for years. This was to be simple. In, out. No *surprises*."

"Yeah, and I'm Moses looking for the right desert—"

A gun clicked behind Lara's ear. "Drop your weapon, Moses. Or lose your head."

Chapter Four

Armand's pilot stepped from behind Lara, his shoulder blood soaked from a bullet wound, his pistol prodding the middle of her back.

Slowly, she released Novak and held her hands up, leaving her gun dangling from her fingertips. Novak jerked himself away and stood. He grabbed her gun, prodded her belly with its barrel.

On the second jab, a tiny wisp of fear circled her heart.

"Looks like I'm the one with the dilemma now."

Before Lara could react, Novak backhanded her across the face, sending her sprawling. Stars exploded behind her eyes, scraped the inside of her skull. With a deliberate pause, she spit the grit from her mouth, then sat up. Tasting the bite of metal, she wiped the blood from her lip.

"It's my turn to ask the questions, Moses."

"I don't talk to dead people," Lara taunted.

Anton Novak's lips curled into a feral grin. "Oh,

I can see this is going to be fun." He turned to the pilot. "See to your boss. We still have a deal to finish."

The pilot nodded and headed for the back of the trailer.

Novak crouched, this time his hand gripped Lara's hair. "Don't I know you?"

The shadows blurred Novak's features, so Lara knew her own were no more distinguishable. "I haven't been slumming lately."

Swearing, Novak raised his closed fist.

"I wouldn't do that if I were you." The order came from behind Novak, its tone clipped and menacing.

Lara's gaze snapped around in time to see Ian.

"Are you okay?" he asked calmly, but the anger was there, seething under the surface of the man. Hot enough that she could almost feel the sand liquefy beneath her.

"Yes." Lara jerked to her feet, using the momentum to place a well-aimed elbow to Novak's gut. His breath whooshed and he dropped to his knees. A wicked smile curved her lips, despite the soreness. "Next time, be a gentleman." She turned to Ian. "The pilot?"

"Dead." The word was short, to the point. Ian studied her for a moment, ignoring Novak. "How long will the buyer be out?"

"Half hour, max." Pain radiated through her ribs from where Novak had shot her. Grimly, Lara rubbed her chest, grateful for her body armor. She'd have a hell of a bruise but not much more.

"How—"

"Later." Ian patted Novak down, discovering a pen-sized cylinder in his pocket.

"Look what I found." He tossed the miniature oxygen canister to Lara. "It recycles a person's carbon monoxide back into oxygen."

Ian grabbed Novak by the collar. "You knew she was coming?"

"Not me." Lara answered for Novak, then scanned the perimeter. "But someone."

A high-pitched whine, faint but distinct cut through the night air.

"Hit the deck!" Ian yelled. The explosion swallowed his warning, spitting it back in a bursting ball of fire and white-hot debris.

Ian dropped Novak midstride and dived into Lara, catching her in a side tackle that sent her flying.

Blast on blast surged over them, raising dirt, shattering the air.

Lara waited for the ground to settle, then shook her head. The after-buzz faded from behind her ears.

"Get off me, hotshot." Lara wiggled to emphasize her point. "I mean it—" She stopped, felt the slack in his muscles, the deadweight on her back.

"Ian! Oh, God, Ian." Lara leveraged her shoulder against the ground, then shifted her hips. "Hold on." Rocks scraped her back, bit into her scalp. But desperation had her ignoring the pain as she worked herself out from beneath him.

Please, don't let him die. Not because of me. She stripped off his mask. "Come on, hotshot! Talk to me," she yelled. She pushed at his shoulder and hip until he rolled over. "Come on." She placed her ear to his heart, heard the steady rhythm beneath her cheek. Relieved, she glanced at his face, tapped it with gentle fingers. "Wake up!"

"I'm up, sweetheart," he murmured. "So you can stop shouting at me. I'm stunned, not deaf." Ian groaned, then rubbed the back of his head. "Must've caught some flying debris." Slowly, he sat up, looked around. "I'm going to kill that son of a bitch."

Novak. An engine revved and Lara swore. The sedan, with Novak behind the wheel, sped off, gravel and dirt clouding the headlight beams.

As she turned back to Ian, she caught sight of the briefcase lying ten feet away.

Lara didn't waste time on arguing. She grabbed the case, then boosted Ian up using her frame to support his and staggered to where darkness rimmed the site.

"Well," Lara commented, as she stared at the burning inferno. "This sucks."

"Who the hell fired that rocket?" Ian asked while he surveyed the fire. With the right coordinates, the launcher could be a mile away.

"I don't know. It doesn't make sense. Neither man would risk blowing up the rig. Not with one boss inside and the other owning the merchandise inside."

Lara shrugged herself out of his embrace and showed Ian the briefcase. "Maybe the answer is in here."

"It wasn't worth your life." Ian half sat, half leaned against a small boulder. Lara curbed the urge to get close again. To feel the reassurance of his body next to hers.

"If you do something like this again, you'll answer to me."

"Is that a threat? Because if it is, you'll have to do better to scare me." Lara surveyed the area. Only the driver's body hadn't been destroyed by the fire. Lara walked over to him and went through his pockets. After a moment, she came up empty.

Ian sighed and shrugged off his gear. "I don't think anything scares you. That's most of your problem." He snagged the infrared binoculars and scanned the perimeter to make sure their company had given up on them. "Our friend is long gone."

"He's not *our* anything." Lara turned, grabbed the briefcase and stalked away. "He's *my* problem."

"Don't you even want to know why I'm here?"

"Nope. I'm angry enough that you are," she snapped, not breaking her stride. "Any time you try to help me with my problems, I end up with worse problems." *Like an unwanted pregnancy.* "So do me a favor and just go away, before I kill you."

"Frankly, Red, I'd thought you'd be more appreciative," he said, not bothering to follow.

"Why? Because the infamous *Orion*—" Lara

sneered Ian's code name "—let my one lead go?" She looked over her shoulder. The flames from the fire cast him in an eerie light, making his features all angles, sharp and hollow. "Drop dead." She turned back and continued walking.

"I let him go to save you."

"Thank you." Lara waved a careless hand in the air. "Don't do me any more favors." She glanced at the stars. Thought briefly about wishing on one for the first time in her life. Then automatically discarded the idea as nonsense. "Could my day get any worse?"

"If you're heading for your SUV, you're wasting time."

Slowly, she swung back. "Why?"

"It has four flat tires."

"Four flat—" Definitely worse.

"Good thing for you, I just happen to have a Hummer sitting about a quarter mile away. Interested?" he invited with a lazy arrogance.

"Of all the dirty—" She bit off the words, and for a moment stared into the darkness, forcing herself to draw in three long, deep breaths. Only after—when she'd calmed down a bit—did she answer. "Do I have a choice?"

"No, you don't."

Her nerve ends crackled while her mind ran through the complications Ian brought with his appearance. With reluctance, she started back toward him. "How did you know where to find me?"

"I followed you from the church. Then after, when you hightailed it out here." He paused, considering. "And with no *Katts Smeart,* or am I mistaken?"

The fact that she hadn't made his tail irked her more than the flat tires. If she hadn't been distracted with the baby—his baby… "You're not. There was a hiccup in the plan."

"Some hiccup. The desert is a long way from Norfolk and headquarters, Red."

He'd said headquarters. A muscle twitched in her jaw. "Cain told you about my operation?"

"That's not all he told me." The bonfire lit the area, giving Lara clear sight of Ian's gaze, pausing deliberately on her stomach.

"Cain has a big mouth." And she'd deal with it later, she vowed. "It's not your baby."

"Liar."

Realizing her hand lay protectively over her belly, she jerked it away, balled it into a fist. "Damn it, Ian. This is exactly why I didn't want you to know yet."

"Then you were going to tell me." Sarcasm saturated the air between them.

His attitude, his problem. She had her own to deal with. "Yes. But only after I had a chance to absorb it and figure out what I'm going to do."

"You sound like you have a choice." Two quick, masculine strides ate the distance between them. He grabbed her by the shoulders, his grip flexing with indecision on whether to shake her or not. "What are you going to do?"

"I don't know," Lara snapped back. "Adoption maybe. Considering our lifestyles."

"Let me tell you something," he snarled. "I don't like this pregnancy any better than you do. But never once did I consider walking away." He brought her closer until only millimeters separated them. "And by God, neither will you."

"What I do is my decision. I've had a little over twenty-four hours to deal with this. And it's not like this baby was conceived in love." She paused, absorbing the ache that slipped through her. "It was in anger, Ian."

"Your anger, not mine."

"Either way, this baby should've never happened." Fear filled her—not the natural adrenaline rush that came with risk, but the instinct for survival. It was sheer terror that rose from her toes, poured out her skin in a cold, clammy sweat.

It was easier to deal with an insane priest, than the possibility of raising a child.

"Well, it did. So let's start there."

"No, let's not. I only have time for one problem right now and it happens to be saving a few hundred people from dying," Lara said, her finger jabbing her point into his chest. "I think that should get my full attention, don't you?"

For a moment he didn't say anything, but Lara knew him well enough that it took effort. "All right."

He bit out the agreement, his hands loosened. "We'll solve your problem first. *Together.* Then we'll deal with the future."

"Fine," Lara said, knowing she had little choice. Ian was the best damn tracker in the business. Better to know where he was at all times than to keep looking over her shoulder.

She stepped back, acknowledging the wave of relief when she'd put some distance between them. "But no one else gets involved. Not Cain, not Kate. No one." Her gaze found his. "I want your word, Ian."

"Since when do you trust my word? Or did you forget how that baby got in your belly in the first place?"

No she hadn't forgotten. But she'd tried. "That was personal, this is business."

"Don't kid yourself, Red. It was all business."

Her breath hissed—the painful jab catching her off guard.

Ian noticed it, was close enough to see the bottle green of her eyes shatter. Regret hit him, low and mean. He'd never treated anyone this bad, especially a woman. His parents had raised him better. But damn it, Lara got under his skin.

Ever since he'd been a young boy, Ian had a knack for reading people at a glance—a trait he inherited from his mother. Lara was the exception. He'd never in his life read someone so wrong. "Fine. You want my word, you have it." The words ground out through gritted teeth.

"Good," she said, the word stiff and lifeless. "One more thing. The second you start throwing threats at me again about this baby, I disappear. And I don't care how good you are, you won't find me."

Chapter Five

Anton Novak glanced up to the rearview mirror, eyeing the fire that raged in the distance.

The loss of merchandise had been necessary. After all, sacrifices had to be made. At least not all the crates had been full. A few explosives—mostly grenades and land mines. Enough to help with the explosion.

In fact, most underneath had lain empty. It would have been bad business to waste more than what Armand would've seen in the open.

His gaze dropped to the digital compass readout on the dash. Northeast. Good. It shouldn't be long now.

Anton eased back into the seat, loosened his fingers on the wheel. Normally, he enjoyed the simple pleasure in driving—something he rarely did anymore.

Now that the operation had been set in motion, it would be a while before he relaxed again.

Within a half mile, Anton caught the distinct flashes of light. He brought the car to a stop.

The door opened and a man slid in beside him. "Well?" the man asked.

Anton noted how the old priest had to use both hands to shut the passenger door. "Are you okay, Father?"

"Just tired," Father Xavier wheezed. He grabbed a handkerchief from his pocket and coughed into it.

"Are you sure?" Anton asked, knowing blood now covered the cloth.

"Yes, yes." The priest nodded impatiently, but still each breath came with difficulty. "It's the dust. And the strain." With a sigh, he settled his head back against the seat rest and closed his eyes.

Anton glanced over, unable to stop the concern. Each day it seemed the other man's skin became thinner, almost papery. Now, its paler hue was visible even in the darkness. They were running out of time.

"Did you destroy the rocket launcher?" Anton asked, surprised when the older man jerked.

"Yes. I had to use several grenades."

"No worries. I have more than enough," Anton joked, but this time he kept his voice low, not wanting to startle the priest again.

"I know," Father Xavier responded, his tone weary. "Tell me what happened."

"She had help," Anton said, wanting to get the worst over. Anton didn't like to disappoint him, but sometimes… "A man. Most likely another operative." He automatically reached for the pack of cigarettes on the dashboard, then stopped. The urge to smoke collided with the need to protect the man beside him.

Sighing, Anton placed both hands on the wheel. "At first, I wasn't so sure we'd succeeded. You'd said Eos was good but Armand's pilot survived her initial attack, then got the drop on her. If he'd killed her outright—"

"But he didn't," Father Xavier inserted.

"No he didn't. Her partner took care of the pilot. Everything else went according to the plan."

"I told her to tell no one."

"Obviously, she didn't listen." Anton paused, remembering the woman's surprise when the man spoke. "Or she didn't know he was coming."

"Either way, I warned her."

"And now?"

"Now, it's in God's hands," Father Xavier murmured, but didn't open his eyes. "Did you recognize her?"

"No. The shadows kept her features hidden. Then the man came up from behind me." Anton remembered her, though—the low, angry brush of her voice when she threatened him, the feminine cry when he'd hit her. "Don't worry, when the time is right we'll discover who she is. And the man, too."

"We're running out of time, Anton," Xavier whispered, his words barely audible now, weakened by exhaustion. "And we must…not…fail."

Anton looked over, heard the uneven rasping and knew from experience the old man was already asleep.

"We won't, Father," he whispered and once again thought of the woman called Eos. "I promise."

THE INTERIOR LIGHT in the Hummer cast a muted beam on the passenger seat. Lara ran her hands over the briefcase's smooth leather surface, searching for any anomalies.

"Here," Ian drew a nonmetal, polymer wire from the cuff of his sweater. "Use this to pick the lock."

"I have one, thanks. I'm more worried about a miniature explosive in the catch." Lara took her time giving the briefcase another once-over.

"The miniatures are Kate's new toys. She hasn't shared them with the rest of our friends," Ian said, using slang for the Bureau and Central Intelligence.

"Actually she gave me one to test…." Satisfied, Lara snapped the catch. "It wasn't locked."

Lara raised the lid and let out a long, slow whistle. "There has to be a million dollars worth of Ben Franklins in here."

"Must be the going rate for a military cache." Ian put the wire away, then started the engine. "Let's have the details, Red."

"I'm sure Cain briefed you." She snapped the lid shut and turned off the overhead light but not before she caught his profile. Shadowed with a night's growth of whiskers, Ian's features sharpened, his expression dangerous.

Desire brushed the base of her spine. Uncomfortable, Lara shifted.

"Cain brought me up to speed on the players and the handoff." Ian reached under his seat. "But I think you need to fill in the rest." He dangled Father Xavier's rosary from his fingers. "Starting with how long you've been Catholic."

"I'm not and you know it." She grabbed the rosary from him. "How did you get into the car?"

Ian pulled out his cell phone, wiggled it back and forth. "My super decoder phone. It scans the mechanism, runs a series of electronic codes. And presto, not only does it unlock the door, but it starts the engine." Ian put it back in his pocket. "It's a Kate D'Amato original. And it beats the hell out of the cereal box super decoder rings."

"Grow up." Lara's eyebrow arched with disgust, but acknowledged the fact that Kate hadn't passed her one. "You had no right breaking in and searching my car, Ian."

"Really? And in my place, you wouldn't have?"

He had a point, but tonight she wasn't in the mood to keep score. "Did you at least grab my duffel and the equipment bag when you were done?"

"Back there," Ian jabbed a thumb toward the seat behind them. "I'm interested in knowing why you'd bring half the tech lab with you when you're on a courier operation."

"Kate gave them to me," Lara replied. "Cain must have told her of my pregnancy. And with Kate being six months pregnant, her mothering instincts went into overdrive. When she kept piling on the equipment, I wasn't about to argue with her."

Ian grunted his understanding. His sister had brought nesting to a whole new level.

"After, I went right from headquarters to the airport."

"Okay, so…" Ian prompted.

"Father Xavier is holding the biochemical weapon as hostage."

"And his terms?"

"I'm to deliver Anton Novak to him within the next—" she glanced at the dash, found the clock "—thirty-seven hours."

"Or?"

"Or Father Xavier will release the chemical into the public."

"A priest willing to murder?"

"You forget this is no ordinary priest."

"Still," Ian paused, considering. "It could be a hell of a bluff."

Lara gripped the cross tighter. If it was, the priest played it well. There was no possible way for her to test the cross without going back to headquarters. After leaving the church, she'd taken no chances and immediately washed it clean.

"Maybe." Lara remembered the regret in Father Xavier's voice, the hollowed sadness. "But there's no way to be sure. And if I warn anyone, he won't wait the thirty-seven hours to release the toxin."

"Exactly what kind of toxin are we dealing with?"

"A synthetically enhanced version of the Red Tide."

"Red Tide? As in toxic oysters?"

"Yes. When the victim ingests the infected shellfish, the toxin is released and attacks the nervous system. Death occurs from asphyxiation or respiratory paralysis. Sometimes within hours."

"How did Davidenko's people enhance the poison?"

"You no longer have to ingest it," Lara answered. "You need only touch it. The skin absorbs the substance and slowly processes it throughout the body."

"So if someone is contaminated, all they have to do is touch another's skin to expose them," Ian reasoned aloud. "How do we stop it?"

"Some biochemical agents degrade when exposed to light, heat or oxygen. The *Katts Smeart* degrades when exposed to antibacterial soap. When someone comes in contact with the agent, all they have to do is wash the exposed skin or contaminated object with an antibacterial soap and warm water to kill the strain. It stops the spread to others."

"Antibacterial soap? Seems simple. Too simple. Why not apply something harsher, like bleach?" Ian tapped the steering wheel, a short staccato, that rode Lara's nerves.

"Harsher chemicals like bleach only serve to open the skin's pores, allowing the poison to seep faster." She reached over, stopped his fingers and instantly realized her mistake. The slide of her head against his tickled her pulse points making them jump to attention. Quickly, she yanked her hand back, but not before she caught the wry twist on Ian's lips.

"There is no other way to pass it. Not airborne, not through body fluids?" he asked, ignoring what had just happened.

"No, it has to be ingested or absorbed in its purest form. After the body processes the poison, the agent breaks down." Lara closed her eyes against the pounding in her temples. What did the doctor say? Aspirin wasn't good for the baby. Absently, she rubbed the side of her forehead, only to stop, startled when she realized her decision not to take aspirin.

"How long will someone have once they've become contaminated?" Ian asked, breaking into her thoughts.

She opened her eyes. "It depends on how much they come in contact with. A little over a tablespoon and they'd be dead within a half hour. A smaller portion—anywhere from four to seventy two hours—depends on the amount. And, of course, a smaller amount increases the chance of survival with the antidote."

"There's an antidote?"

"Father Xavier says there is," Lara admitted. "I haven't seen it."

"So we only have the word of a priest that it exists."

"A priest who has gone rogue." Lara caught Ian's frown.

"And you have no idea why the priest wants Novak?"

"No," Lara answered, finding no logical reason to tell Ian she'd been infected. They had enough to deal with. "But Château Bontecou was no random choice for a meeting. Davidenko owns it."

"Does the priest know who you are, what you look like?"

"No. Of course not, but—"

"And Novak? Do you think he got a good look at you in the desert?"

"He could have but I doubt it," Lara explained. "I could barely make out his features when we tangled. Either way, we're forced to chance it. I need Novak."

"You do remember the fact that he was ready for you, Red?"

"Even if he was, it doesn't matter. We're running out of time. And options."

"Not if it means another trap." Ian glanced from Lara to the briefcase, then he threw the Hummer into drive. "I think we should take advantage of Novak's generosity first."

Lara raised an eyebrow. "What do you have in mind?"

"Everyone knows with gambling the odds favor

the house," Ian stated. "But I think we're about to change their luck."

CHÂTEAU BONTECOU, like most casinos, advertised their winners in a loud obnoxious fashion. Bells chimed, horns blew and people clapped.

A loud cry pierced the air.

Some, Ian discovered, even screamed.

His gaze slid to the casino bar's entrance where an elderly woman—one of many seniors—hopped up and down, her ample bosom heaving in excited agitation. In a glance he took in her tangerine pants suit, matching pumps and beehive hairdo. Obviously, the woman liked the fifties so much, she hadn't wanted to leave it, Ian mused. He leaned on the bar and enjoyed the show.

Across the casino floor, a woman wandered into his line of sight. A brunette, her hair dark and bobbed. A white sleeveless blouse, trimmed with a black collar. Modest by most standards—if Lara hadn't left all but the two middle buttons unfastened. The cotton stretched across her breasts, leaving a tantalizing glimpse of the silk and lace beneath.

Flared, pin-striped trousers hung low across her hips, exposing just enough of her stomach to frame a diamond belly ring.

Desire punched him—on its heels a more powerful jab of protectiveness. His baby—their baby—was there, nestled beneath the soft curve of her belly.

Cool green eyes flickered over the crowd, once,

twice before they settled into a lazy perusal of his pants and polo shirt. She paused a moment on his expression of warning before she took another long appreciative glance.

Ian let out a hiss of air. He knew what she was doing, and damn it, it was working.

With slow deliberation, Lara sauntered over to him, placed her leather, mini backpack on the bar and slid onto the closest empty stool.

The bartender—Hank, by the nametag—flashed a nice, practiced smile and slid a napkin in front of her. "What can I get you?"

"Shot of whiskey, please." She ran her tongue quick and light over her glossed red lips. Her eyes, lined in a deep smoky gray and fringed with thick black-tipped lashes, shimmered green with amusement. She lowered one lid into a slow, sexy wink. "MacAlister whiskey, if you have it."

She'd ordered his family brand deliberately. Ian stretched in front of her and grabbed a handful of peanuts. "Watch, it, Red," he murmured right before Hank reappeared with a glass.

Once Lara had accused him of putting duty above all else. It hadn't been duty that placed him here.

His eyes ran the length of her.

Not by a frustrating, sexy, long shot.

"Hello, handsome." She swiveled until she faced him then crossed a long, easy leg over the other. "Can I buy you a drink?"

She'd made contact, after agreeing he'd make the first move. Ian suppressed the urge to throttle her delicate neck and instead allowed a lazy smile to play across his lips.

"Absolutely."

Without taking his eyes off her face, he said to Hank, "Same. But make it a double."

Lara's eyebrow quirked in response. "Maggie." She held out her hand.

Ian slid his hand into hers, catching the slight tremble of her palm against his. "Jim. Nice to meet you."

"We'll see." Gently, she tugged her hand free.

When Hank placed the double shot in front of Ian, Lara raised her own. For a moment he watched the track lights catch and set the gold liquid on fire. "A toast, Jim," she purred.

A tickle of warning danced across Ian's shoulder blades. He raised his glass.

"To—"

"Excellent whiskey," he drawled.

"All right," she agreed, then lifted a casual shoulder.

Not waiting, he tipped the glass toward hers—heard the clink of promise. Over the rim, he watched Lara fake a sip before tipping hers onto the carpet.

So, she wasn't drinking. Because of the mission or the baby?

Ian downed his drink in one gulp, felt the bite,

then the burn before he slid the glass back onto the counter. With a casual nod, he caught the bartender's eye and gave a slight shake of his head. Hank had been behind the counter long enough to know that there was better money if he left them alone.

Ian leaned into Lara, whispered in her ear. "Ready?"

Lara's laugh held the edge of seduction, her finger lightly tapped Ian's lips—an intimate gesture to any onlooker. "Too soon. I don't want to appear that easy," she whispered, her tone husky with promise.

"Easy?" Ian nuzzled her ear, allowed himself to breathe in her fragrance. She smelled of ginger with the faint hint of jasmine. The delicate scent stole through him, then settled deep in his gut. "You?"

Lara had never been one to wear the same scent. Hell, she couldn't even buy the same brand of shampoo twice in a row.

"You're a lot of things," he murmured against the shell of her ear, pleased when he felt the slight shiver of her shoulders. "Arrogant, bossy…" He paused, his lips tasted her delicate lobe "…extremely sexy. But you're *not* easy."

"And," she whispered and pulled away until they were nose to nose. "I'm not ready."

"Okay," he murmured. Vulnerability dimmed the shimmer in Lara's eyes. The air shifted between them, like a slow-moving pendulum, swinging dangerously close to personal. "Hold on."

Lara watched as Ian strolled over to a nearby

jukebox. He'd traded the black sweater for a gray polo shirt that molded snug around his broad shoulders and exchanged his pants for a pair of navy Dockers. He'd left the shirt untucked in typical Ian-fashion. That combined with a day's growth of whiskers, gave him that sexy, go-to-hell appearance.

A dangerous combination. One that turned Lara's nerves into a handful of Mexican jumping beans.

Across the empty dance floor, drifted the deep, pulsating, Etta James rendition of "At Last!" Lara closed her eyes, letting the words seep in, the mournful melody soothing the erratic tempo that thrummed throughout her body.

"Want to dance?"

Lara opened her eyes, saw his eyebrow arch in challenge. Chin hiked, she placed her hand in his, felt his callused fingers brush against her palm.

With her second step, she was in his arms, snug against the hardness of his body. One hand splayed across the small of her back, his fingers absently stroking, reassuring. The other held hers clasped between them.

"That was a dirty trick, Ian." Her tone strived for haughty, but fell way short. Etta James was a weakness she'd shared with him the night she'd grieved for her father.

"I don't have time to court you. We need to get close, quick. The more we play up our attraction, the less camera time our faces will have."

"Fine." The song lasted what? Two minutes. She sighed, snuggled in. Keep it simple. In the poignant, sadness of the music, she found an escape.

Without thought, she breathed in the clean scent of soap, hummed the tune against the hollow of his neck.

Allowed both to seep through, settle within.

"We're doing fine. Drawing just the right amount of attention."

"Hmmmm." Lara floated, drugged by the low, whiskey-soaked voice in her ear and the slow, pulsing music surrounding her. Her lips skimmed Ian's jaw, enjoyed the simple tang that touched off a long-forgotten craving for the spice underneath.

Not knowing who made the move, not caring. Lara sighed when his mouth met hers. From that moment, Ian took control.

Then her mind shut down, stopped thinking about the operation—urged by the sensual lure of his mouth. With a whimper, Lara opened, tasted—then like an addict she saturated herself in the thick, sultry heat. The kind conjured from smoky dives with dark corners.

When he started to pull away, she clamped down on the taut muscles of his arms. Felt them flex with indecision. "More." Her order sliced through the low murmur of voices, effectively cutting off all sound.

The music had stopped.

The thrum of yearning, the rush of moisture between her thighs unsettled her. But it was the humiliation that heated her face, made her eyes tear. *Damn it!*

"Maggie?"

The name snapped her chin up, brought reality rushing back. But pride straightened her spine, gave her strength. "Yes?"

"Want that drink now?" Ian's breathing was held with a tight, but controlled edge. "I know I could use one."

She nodded, not trusting herself to speak. Ian draped his arm around her shoulders. After a quick squeeze—for reassurance or as a warning, she wasn't sure—Ian led her back to the bar.

Lara slid onto the stool. This time, not so easily, her knees were shaking that bad.

She reached out, grabbed her empty shot glass and placed it in his face. "Buy me another?" Tears welled, her throat spasmed with her effort to hold them in check.

"Don't," he whispered, his tone harsh with puzzlement. In a louder voice he said, "Sure." Then gently took the glass from her hand. "You know, I have better upstairs."

"You do?" She paused, studying him. Using the brief moment to gather her wits. "Why not?" With light fingers, she patted his cheek and grabbed her purse from the bar. "Thanks, Hank." Lara blew him a kiss.

The bartender smiled, but Ian noted the tinge of envy that crossed the older man's features before he pocketed the tip Ian laid on the bar.

"You did that on purpose," Lara murmured.

"Did what?"

"No games. We agreed," she said through clenched teeth.

"No. We agreed that I would take the lead. So that's what I did." He smiled, then kissed her forehead. "Now remember, there are cameras in the elevator."

"I remember," Lara retorted. The ache from their kiss clawed the sides of her belly. She entwined both her arms around one of his and smiled—her expression adoring.

"Don't over do it," he warned quietly through his own smile. "We don't need to set the elevator on fire. We just need to get to our floor."

"Don't tell me how to work."

Château Bontecou centered on Davidenko's recreation of the River Cher. Limestone archways spanned the river, dividing the Château into two separate palaces—the casino and the hotel.

Mindful of the cameras, they both kept their heads together, their faces shadowed. Taking their time, Lara and Ian crossed the Atrium Bridge which led from the casino to the hotel.

"Almost there, sweetheart," Ian coaxed.

Laughing lightly, she pulled him into an empty elevator.

Ian eased into her, his body hard, his hand spread at the small of her back. Heat slipped through her, warm and liquid. Lara dropped her chin and closed her eyes, willing herself not to get lost again.

But when he shifted closer, murmured nonsense in her ear—the combination of the hard strength and moist undertone nurtured the ache in her loins. Her muscles tightened against the assault.

"Damn it, Red, relax," Ian growled.

The sexy vibration sparked shock waves down her spine, amped up her ache ten decimals. She bit back a moan.

"We're supposed to be into some heavy petting here."

"Then let's do it right," she whispered. With a slight tug on his hair, she pulled his face mere inches from hers, felt his breath shudder out. She licked her lips, anticipating. "For the cameras."

Chapter Six

Lara's lips found Ian's. She tasted the scotch, absorbed its bite, the hint of fruit. Her tongue dipped, teased, coaxing him to participate. She knew what he liked, used it to incite.

"The cameras," Ian murmured. He grabbed the back of her head, held it in place and feasted on her mouth, her neck and when she gasped, her mouth again. Her body trembled, her hand fisted his shirt, this time not taking the chance he'd stop. Not until he'd satisfied.

The elevator doors slid open. Ian pulled back, swore again. Lara took in his hooded lids, the flash of blue heat—felt the latter's blast against her cheeks.

"Let's go," he ordered, desire keeping his words to a low, husky murmur. He grabbed her hand and tugged her behind him. Only sheer willpower kept her moving on shaky legs.

"I'm over here." He nodded down the hallway. "Third room on the right." Within moments, they reached the door. Ian inserted the key, turned the lock. Laughter echoed through the hall. Lara didn't glance up. How in the hell was she going to explain—

"Maggie. Did you hear what I said?"

"What?" She looked up then, caught the tempered steel in Ian's gaze.

"The room. We're here." He took her elbow and guided her through the door, then closed it. "Stay put."

He walked through the room, his eyes on his watch, checking for hidden transmitters.

Father Xavier's room wasn't, by any means, top-of-the-line, Lara decided. It was more of an understated display of cream brocade and dark mahogany. Classic. Refined. She glanced past the love seat, desk and mini bar to the bedroom where she noted its two double beds.

Neither Lara nor Ian expected Father Xavier to put in an appearance so soon. But now, Lara thought, would be a good time.

"It's clear of devices," Ian stated from the bedroom. He walked into the suite. "I checked for transmitters earlier. And again just now. We're set."

"Good." Lara sank onto the love seat. Someone had just pulled her world from under her feet. How was she supposed to stand? She hadn't touched anyone since Ian. *Hadn't the desire,* she thought. Had decided she was done with men for a while.

"Now what the hell happened back there, Red?"

"I was supposed to play a role. I played it." Lara bit the inside of her cheek, trying to absorb this new revelation. The desire had disappeared, simply because Ian had disappeared.

"Wrong. I know when you're acting. And lady, that was no act. A few minutes ago, you were two seconds from naked."

Closer than that. "You're reading too much into it. The baby is…." Lara struggled for the right word. "The doctor warned me…."

"Warned you what?" Ian advanced, concern etched in his features. "Is something wrong with the baby?"

"No." Lara paused, frustration riding every single nerve. "It's my hormones, they're raging."

Ian cocked an eyebrow. "This I have to hear." He leaned against the wall, crossed his arms and tucked his fingers in his armpits.

"Raging is the doctor's word, not mine. But it definitely fits. And sometimes the hormones are hard to control, that's all. When we were dancing…when you whispered next to my ear…I…" Lara shook her head. Annoyed, she reached for the buttons of her blouse, started undoing them one by one. "Just forget it, all right? It's not going to happen again."

"What else are these hormones doing exactly?" Ian asked, but his eyes flared over her wandering hands.

Lara swung away, took off her shirt and turned it inside out, leaving only black showing. "Nothing serious." Ignoring the tremble in her fingers, she slipped her arms in and buttoned the blouse from top to bottom. "Where's my backpack?"

"At the foot of the bed," he said, but his gaze remained fixed with hers. "Are the hormones making you nauseous?"

"No, just queasy with certain smells. Gasoline for one, red meat...sometimes," Lara answered. She yanked off her wig and the hair cap underneath. She tossed both on the bed, then grabbed a black knit ski mask from her pack.

"What else?"

"Nothing, damn it." After pulling on the cap, she jammed the stray tendrils inside.

"Lara, I'm not going to stop until—"

"Fine." She nearly shouted the word. "I cry."

"You? Cry?"

She might as well have drawn her pistol and shot him, his expression was that dumbfounded. "Is that so hard to believe?"

"Frankly, yes," Ian admitted, amused. "You're the last person on earth—"

"Shut up, Ian." Lara grabbed his black T-shirt from her pack and threw it at him. Insensitive jerk.

Ian pulled his polo over his head and tossed it on the bed. Lara's belly clenched at the play of light across the width of his shoulders. She tried not to remember the feel of them tightening beneath her hands when he climaxed.

"Look, Red, I'm sorry—"

"No, you're not." She rolled his shirt up and shoved it into the mini backpack. "But you will be if you don't drop this now," she warned. The wig and its cap followed the polo into the bag.

"Where's the equipment?"

"Out on the balcony with my backpack. All but the transmitter." Ian pulled a small case from his pocket, tossed it like a coin in the air. "Didn't want to lose it." Suddenly, his eyes found hers in the mirror. "Raging, huh?"

"Ian…"

"What?"

"Go to hell."

Thursday, 0300 hours

ANTON NOVAK CONSIDERED the Château Bontecou a French architectural masterpiece surrounded by marble courtyards, award-winning gardens and an acre-wide maze of bushes and interlocking bricks.

The Château had taken Davidenko five years to build and cost millions of dollars in financing. But Anton knew that it was worth every minute, every penny—every drop of sweat that went into its birth.

"Good morning, Mr. Novak."

"Good morning, Maurice." Anton held his hand up in greeting, but continued past the concierge to Davidenko's private elevator. After a brief nod for two security guards, he walked onto the elevator and pressed the button for Davidenko's suite.

For the first time in a long time, Anton felt the snap

of nerves along his spine. He frowned, imagining betrayal would do that to a man. Even if the reason was sound, the act itself, was a new experience.

With a sigh, he understood the betrayal couldn't be helped. But it did not ease his conscience.

He deliberately didn't stop at his own apartment, wanting Davidenko to see the grime-ridden suit, now ruined after the scuffle with Eos.

The door slid open and Anton stepped out into the grand entryway. He was met by yet another man, Joseph. Davidenko's personal enforcer.

"Hello, Mr. Novak."

"Hello, Joseph." Anton automatically raised his arms for the search. It didn't matter if Anton was the closest thing Davidenko had to a son, Davidenko didn't trust anyone.

And Joseph, Anton understood, shared the same opinion. The enforcer trusted no one, least of all Anton.

Then again, Anton couldn't blame the man.

Anton lost his mother at the age of five. With his father unable to care for him, he had been shuffled from foster parent to foster parent until, at the age of nine, he'd escaped to the streets. Over the years, he'd perfected a talent for pickpocketing. By twelve he'd become one of the best on the street.

One night, he marked Davidenko, a rich man new to the Las Vegas streets. He'd performed the bump and roll to perfection. Running, as if someone had been chasing him, he bumped into Davidenko, snatched the wallet, then took off.

Once Davidenko discovered his wallet missing, he sent Joseph after the thief with specific orders to kill.

"Thank you, Mr. Novak," Joseph said, forcing Anton's thoughts to the present. The enforcer stepped back. Over six feet tall, there wasn't a scrap of unused muscle in the two-hundred-fifty pound frame. Many times over the years Anton wondered what might have happened if Joseph had found him on that fateful day.

"They called from downstairs. Mr. Davidenko is expecting you."

"Thanks, Joseph." Anton's smiled widened. There had been a good reason Joseph had never found Anton. On the street nothing stayed a secret. Soon, Anton knew he was marked for killing. Instead of waiting, he sought a meeting with Davidenko, returned the wallet and its contents, then offered his services.

Davidenko had taken a liking to Anton. Pickpockets, Anton had learned, garnered much respect in the Russian world of crime. By the time Joseph returned empty-handed, Anton had become Davidenko's personal errand boy.

Something Joseph never forgot, Ian mused, then entered Davidenko's private quarters.

Dubbed the blue suite by the staff, Davidenko's apartment was no different from the rest of the hotel. Each had the stamp of French Renaissance splendor.

Elegant, immaculate. The coffered ceiling, if studied closely, revealed an intertwining *M* and *D*. Arrogantly inspired from past century kings. The walls dripped with French and Italian masterpieces. Veronese. Tintoretto. Monet.

The furniture consisted mostly of fifteenth century walnut and marble. All accented in dusty blue brocade and velvet drapes.

Only two changes disrupted the French ambience. A wall of monitors—all tapped into the different areas of the hotel and casino—and a ten-foot fish tank behind the bar.

"Anton, come in."

Business did make strange bedfellows, Anton noted. "Hello, Mr. Davidenko."

Whimpers floated on the air. Anton glanced at the monitor already guessing what he'd see—a woman strapped to the chair, her arms bound. Behind her stood a man with a black wand twirling in his hands.

"A Taser?"

"Beatings have proved to be ineffective in the past." Davidenko hit an intercom button. "Take her to her suite and leave her there. The doctor will be up shortly to take care of the rest."

"Auction?" Anton asked. One of the men grabbed Sophia Franco by the arm and hoisted her over his shoulder.

"No, she's too well-known."

"If you sold her body parts, you'd get more money," Anton reasoned. Bile coated his tongue. With effort, he swallowed it back.

Davidenko walked over to the bar and poured himself a double vodka. He didn't offer Anton a drink but then again, Anton had worked long enough for Davidenko that he didn't expect one.

"No. I won't dissect her." Davidenko shrugged. "Call me sentimental."

"Did you find out what she did with the poison?"

"She denied taking it," Davidenko said, then set the bottle down.

"And the chemists' notes?"

"That, too."

"That's impossible."

"Improbable, not impossible," Davidenko drawled in Russian. He tipped his glass toward Anton. "What happened to you?"

"Armand is dead. So is my man, Georgy and the truck driver."

"The merchandise?"

"Destroyed."

"I see." Davidenko swallowed the double shot of vodka. "This is not good news, Anton."

"It gets worse."

"Worse?" Davidenko's laugh sounded like steel grinding on vocal cords. The small hairs rose at the base of Anton's neck. "The only thing worse is that you lost my money."

"Whoever killed Georgy, Armand and his men, also blew up the munitions. The money was inside."

"Yet you escaped."

"Yes," Anton agreed evenly, knowing he was balancing on a thin edge.

Davidenko paused. His keen black eyes studied Anton. After a moment his lips curled into an easy smile. "All right, Anton. We'll check into this mishap. I want to know who interfered with our business." He walked over and put his hand on Anton's shoulder, then squeezed. "Then I want you to kill them."

"I had planned on it." The relief rushed through Anton, making him light-headed for a moment. His gamble had paid off. Of course, the odds had been with him. He'd never failed Davidenko in the past, but still…

"Good," Davidenko said, seemingly appeased. Yet the threat was there, laced within the word.

"I will, of course, replace the money I lost. And the merchandise."

"Of course," Davidenko agreed. "But next time, Anton, should this happen again…" Davidenko's eyes narrowed into slits of black. "It would be best you die with your comrades. Understood?"

"Understood."

"WE HAVE TO SAVE HER. We have no choice." Although Lara kept her words low, urgency punctuated each syllable.

Like two bats hiding among the Château's limestone niches, Lara and Ian hung suspended above an arched window, observing Novak's conversation with Davidenko.

"No. We *have* to install this receiver." Ian took in their surroundings with a slow, steady gaze. "Then get the hell off of this wall. We're too exposed hanging here."

"I know," Lara whispered. "But—"

"We'll save the woman. After we plant the transmitter."

"Thanks." Lara smiled, knowing Ian couldn't see it through her mask. She couldn't hear Sophia's whimpering, her screams. But she understood the shock of pain.

Novak and Davidenko continued to talk. Lara tilted her electronic camera farther down the window, aware that every millimeter risked discovery.

"What are they saying?"

"Novak's not happy. He's telling Davidenko that Sophia was the only one capable of stealing the biochemical." Lara paused, waiting for Davidenko to face her more so she could read his lips. A trick she'd picked up in boarding school and had perfected over the years. "Davidenko isn't as sure."

"Someone else could have lifted it out of Davidenko's vault," Ian murmured. "Someone else on the inside."

"Novak?"

Ian grunted softly, but his eyes continued to take in the perimeter. "It wouldn't be the first time the second in command turned. With the right backing, Novak could bring Davidenko down."

"Maxim is backed by the Russian mob. If Novak wanted to take over, he'd have to get more than just Davidenko."

"You mean *Godfather* style? Him at a christening, his men killing the heads of all the families? That happens only in the movies, Red."

"But if he promised the big guys a biochemical? I know for a fact, Davidenko isn't being a good sharer with his new Weapon of Mass Destruction."

"Maybe," Ian appeased. "But to be sure, we're going to have to chat with Miss Franco. For some reason my muse is telling me she might just have the answer we need."

"If she survives."

Carefully, Ian drew out a specialized drill. The size of a one-inch needle, Kate had made the drill small enough to evade detection in the glass, but big enough to hold their booster. "Most monitor systems are hooked up by remote." He inserted the receptor. "This little baby should intercept it and feed it to our computers. Go ahead and check."

Lara turned upright, grabbed her palm-sized computer. A checkerboard of pictures blinked once, then stayed. "Set." She nodded toward the inside. "Let's get Franco."

Ian glanced at the distant ground below. "We can't bring her outside. She wouldn't have the strength to handle the ropes. And it would take too long to bring her down ourselves." On Davidenko's monitor, Lara watched his goons dump Sophia Franco on her bed. The bigger of the two zapped her with the Taser one last time.

"Then..." Lara's response was low and determined. "We'll just have to find another way."

IT TOOK ALMOST A HALF HOUR for them to locate Sophia's suite.

By the time they had, and positioned themselves on the balcony, an older man—probably the doctor—was tucking the coverlet around a now-clean Sophia Franco.

"If he works for Davidenko, he won't report the assault to the authorities," Lara murmured, before adjusting her mask.

They circled around to the other patio door. Just beyond was the living room. The bodyguard, dressed in a dark suit, looked out of place among the delicate cream silks and velvets that made up the living area. He sat on the couch engrossed with a television program. One of the reality shows, Lara noticed.

With cautious fingers, Lara tested the French patio door, pleased when she found it unlocked. "How convenient for us," she whispered.

With a nod, Lara raised her gun. Silently, she

pushed the door open. Under Lara's cover, Ian slipped through the doorway, his feet soundless on the thick, Venetian carpet.

Ian waited to the count of three, then crept up behind the couch. Seconds later, Lara heard the grunt of surprise, the crack of bone and watched the bodyguard slide wordlessly onto his side.

"Reality bites, doesn't it?" she murmured. Lara had no sympathy for the man, recognizing him immediately as one who'd assaulted Sophia Franco with the Taser. Quickly, she hit the switch, dousing the room into darkness.

With a snap, the bedroom door opened and the doctor walked out. The backlight from the bedroom made the doctor's eyesight temporarily impaired.

"Yuri? What's going on?"

Before Ian could react, Lara had stepped behind the doctor—a balding man with slightly stooped shoulders—and placed the gun under his chin. She jammed his head back. The man's Adam's apple bobbed nervously against the steel.

"Yuri's dead. And so are you, if you don't answer some questions," Lara whispered. "What's your name?"

"Moravia. Dr. Edward Moravia. I'm Mikhail Davidenko's personal physician," the man rasped.

"You say that with pride, Doctor. But I can guarantee the fact that you work for Davidenko will not save you from a bullet."

"You hurt me, Mikhail will come after you."

Lara sneered. "I can only hope."

Ian stepped up from the shadows. "What's wrong with the woman in there?"

"Nothing—"

"Remember, bullets kill." Lara jabbed the gun, making sure she caught his larynx with the barrel's tip.

Moravia gasped in pain, but still managed to speak. "She'll die if you don't let me help her."

Ian noted the woman's still form on the bed. "Is she alive?" Ian demanded, his voice hushed but lethal.

"Yes. Barely."

"How many of Davidenko's men are in the hallway, Doctor?"

"One, but there are cameras everywhere. If you give yourselves up now—"

Lara brought the pistol down on the back of the doctor's head.

With a grunt, he dropped to the floor unconscious.

"You took pleasure in that," Ian commented, stepping over the body.

"Damn right I did," Lara answered, then raced into the bedroom. "We have to disarm those cameras for a few minutes. Can you intersect the camera frequency, now that we're hooked up?"

"We're risking the transmitter," Ian admitted, following. "It won't take long for them to find the source of the cameras malfunction. If they do, they'll find our toy."

"We'll just have to take that chance. We're not leaving her." Lara reached the bed. First thing she saw was the plastic stretched out beneath Sophia. Fear skittered over Lara's nerve endings. "They've laid a tarp." Killing someone on plastic, saved time. No messy DNA samples to clean up.

"Who are you?" Sophia asked, her voice so weak Lara placed her face mere inches from the starlet's lips.

"We're friends." Lara knelt next to the bed, took off her glove then grabbed the woman's hand. It was cold, clammy with death. "We're taking you out of here."

"You're too late." A tear slipped down the side of Sophia's temple.

"No—"

"She's right," Ian whispered, then swore. Lara followed his gaze to a tube that ran from Sophia's thigh, through a pump, to an embalming basin on the other side of the bed. "They're draining her blood, the bastards. Pumping her dry through her femoral artery."

"It doesn't matter," Sophia rasped.

Still, Ian pulled the tube. With both hands, he applied pressure to the artery. "We need a tourniquet."

"No," Sophia rasped. "Please."

"Sophia listen to me." Lara's words were urgent, her tone shadowed with sadness. "You have to tell me what happened to the *Katts Smeart.*"

"Gave it to father..." Sophia's eyes fluttered shut. "My baby...mistake."

Lara checked her pulse, then the stillness of her chest. "She's dead," she said flatly.

Beyond the door, Moravia yelled for help.

Ian swore, threw the tube down. "You didn't hit the doctor hard enough."

"Give me another shot at it. He'll stay down this time." Lara stepped past Ian, but he grabbed her arm. In the distance they heard the slam of the door, heard the running feet.

"If they find us in here, it'll be the Alamo all over again."

"Sophia—"

"We can't do anything for her now, damn it." Ian grabbed Lara, hauled her behind him to the patio. A split second later, two men ran in, guns raised. Both were dark and ugly, with ponytailed hair and stone-cut faces. Bodybuilding carbon copies dressed in matching black suits.

"Turn on the light, Viktor." The order jarred the darkness. Both men saw the doctor at the same time. The first man went in search of his comrade, while the other dropped to his knees and shook the doctor.

Outside, Ian swung over the cemented wall, fired. The patio doors exploded. "Go!"

Lara saw the three men dive to the floor. She dropped her clip, shoved in her cable anchor. Gunfire sprayed around her, kicking up bits of concrete. She swung over the wall, pulled the trigger, hearing the thump of the anchor imbedding the cement below the balcony. After one tug, she clipped her harness and let go.

The two guards leaned over the wall, firing. Bullets strafed the limestone and slate above her. Ian emptied his clip, forcing both men to take cover.

Lara ducked, then hit the lever unlocking her harness brake and dived into a free fall. She counted to three, then jerked the brake and stopped six feet above ground. After tilting her gun toward the castle, she glanced down, half expecting security to meet them. When no one appeared, Lara released her harness and hit the ground running.

Chapter Seven

Darkness invaded the maze. The air was thick with the scent of earth and fresh-cut branches, the sweet hint of roses. Lara came to a stop, taking in oxygen in huge deep gulps. "Damn it." After a moment, she grabbed the ski mask from her head, shook her hair free of the bun.

Ian appeared behind her, his footsteps soundless. "That was close."

"Too close." Quickly, they stripped down to the shorts they wore beneath. Lara tied the ends of her blouse high up under her breasts. She reached for Ian's backpack, pulled out a yellow T-shirt and threw it to him before shoving the pants into the pack.

Ian tossed it back. "I'll keep this one on."

"Why?" Before he could stop her, she pulled down the neck of his shirt, saw the line of blood where the bullet creased his skin. "You're hurt."

"It's just a scratch. I caught some flying cement

on the way down. But the blood will show through the lighter shirt."

The copper scent of blood caught in her nose. Lara took a deep breath through her mouth.

"What is it?"

"I don't—" A wave of nausea rolled through her. She tried to recover, but another crashed over the first.

"What's the matter?"

"Nothing. Just a little sick." Automatically, she shook her head, then realized her mistake. This time her stomach heaved in protest. "The blood. It's making me nauseous. Can't deal with raw meat or chicken anymore, either." Lara dug into her shorts pocket and brought out a piece of peppermint candy.

"A little—" Ian swore, but a protective arm went around her nonetheless. "When was the last time you ate or slept?"

"Yesterday," she said, not minding that he yelled, as long as he didn't move. She gripped his arm tighter just to make sure he didn't. The mint soothed, then stopped the queasiness.

"Did it occur to you to sleep or eat on the plane out here?"

"It occurred to me. But it didn't seem like a good idea since I piloted my Cessna out here," she commented, then forced her body to relax. She took a deep breath, giving the world a chance to right itself. Finally, she felt strong enough to step away from Ian.

"I didn't think to eat at the time. I was angry, if you must know. At you."

"You're always mad at me—have been for months. That never stopped you from eating before."

"You've got to be kidding. There's quite a bit of difference between being pissed off about your code name and being pregnant with your baby." Of all the stupid attitudes…

"Get over it, Red. Then eat something," Ian ordered.

"You make it sound like I'm starving myself on purpose, Ian," she said, exasperation melding now with anger. "I've been a little busy."

"You're not helping anybody, if you don't take care of yourself."

"A woman is dead up there. They killed her," she snapped. "If I'd been thinking a little bit more about the mission—"

"She'd still be dead and a hundred other people might be, too."

Lara sat on the bench, the weight of the world suddenly pressing in. Ian sat beside her, gathered her close. "There was nothing we could do, Red. He'd tapped into a major artery—"

Ian stopped, put his finger up and snagged his gun from its ankle holster.

"Yo! Hand over your paper!"

Lara jump up and swung around, fists raised. Even in the dark, she saw two teenage boys, dressed in droopy jeans and oversize T-shirts. She forced her muscles to relax. "Paper?" Lara asked, confused.

"Coin, bitch. Cash."

"Watch your mouth," Ian ordered. "And get lost. This is a private party." Ian shoved his weapon back into the ankle holster and spared no more than a glance at the two teenagers holding knives. In his current mood, he didn't trust himself not to shoot them.

One of teens stood back and let the skinnier of the two take the lead.

Obviously, they didn't see the gun. Snot-nosed brats wanting cash for a quick fix or bragging rights to their friends. "There's nothing but trouble here," he advised, his tone hard.

"Shut the hell up," the leader said.

Ian pinched the bridge of his nose. "I don't have time for this."

"They're kids, Ian. Don't you dare take your anger out on them."

"Who you calling a kid, bitch?" The huskier of the two puffed out his chest, then flashed his switchblade. "Shut the hell up or I'll carve your pretty *chica* face."

Lara raised an eyebrow. *Chica* meant girl in Spanish. Right? Lucky for them, she wasn't sure.

"That's it," Ian warned. "I'm counting to three. If you aren't gone by then, you're going to need a hospital. Got me?"

"Yeah, I got you, Pops. Right here." Skinny grabbed his crotch and laughed.

"Ian," Lara warned. "Don't, they're just...expanding their horizons."

Ian snorted. "Into what? Grand larceny?"

"I told you to be quiet, bitch." The leader stepped forward, underestimating Lara's frustration and her reach. She kicked out, hitting the boy's wrist. He screamed and dropped the knife.

She turned to Ian. "See. No harm done."

The huskier teen threw his knife. Ian blocked it with his backpack. When the knife hit the ground. Ian glanced from it to the boy. "Well?"

The boy froze. Ian sighed, scooped up the blade and turned his back on the kid. "Damn it, Red. Is this your idea of how to handle teenagers?"

"I'm not having this conversation with you—"

"Watch out," Ian ordered.

With a yell, Skinny launched himself at Lara. She sidestepped, stuck out her foot and shoved with her shoulder. He tripped into a nearby rosebush. His howls rent the air.

"For God's sake, they're just thorns," she snapped, her own patience worn thin. With a quick glance she took in the scratches across his face and arms, decided he'd survive.

"Are you guys finished?" Ian asked, his tone disdainful, his fingers twirling the switchblade—deciding if it was worth Lara's fury to beat some sense into the boys.

Suddenly, the first one grabbed his friend and yanked. "We're outta here. You all are crazy."

Skinny grabbed his knife from the ground and Ian watched both boys run down the path. Satisfied they wouldn't be back, he handed Lara the switch-blade. "Here. A souvenir."

Lara sighed and took the knife, flipped the blade back into its handle and tucked it into her pocket. "Thank you for not hurting them."

"Don't thank me, because if I see them again—" Ian bit off the sentence. Instead, he glanced up for patience and let out a long, labored sigh. "We've got to get going. It's almost dawn."

Lara followed his gaze, noting the violet-pink-tinted sky. "Ian, Sophia said she'd given the formula to Father Xavier. There's a good chance Davidenko had made a copy. I'm going into Davidenko's office. If he has a copy, it's on his computer hard drive. If I can manage to download it, even if Father Xavier exposes these people, we'll be able to save them."

"*We're* going into Davidenko's office."

"Not this time, hotshot," Lara corrected. "This time the job calls for a woman."

Thursday, 0900 hours

"MOVE IT, RED."

"I'm almost there," she whispered, knowing her earpiece would pick up her voice loud and clear for

Ian on the other end. She glanced at the elevator's monitor and counted the floors. Only seven more to go to Davidenko's apartment.

It had taken longer than Lara had expected to slip into the service area of the hotel unnoticed.

Once inside, though, she searched for the ladies' locker room. Cameras were unlikely where the women dressed. Even so, Lara kept her features hidden whenever possible.

She broke into a locker, grabbed a uniform and passkey, then located a laundry bin and filled it with cleaning supplies.

The service elevator doors dinged, then slid open. She glanced at her watch. Five minutes until nine.

With a quick shove, she maneuvered the bin out into the foray.

"Who are you?"

Lara stopped, seemingly startled. She recognized the hired goon, had seen him in Sophia's room.

In four quick strides, he was in her face. "I said, who are you?"

One look into the clear, black eyes, told Lara he had more than his fair share of intelligence.

"Vivian." She pointed to her stolen name tag. "I am the housekeeper. The…maid," Lara answered, her words thick with a Spanish accent. "I am here to clean."

Earlier, she'd lifted a blank schedule sheet from a storeroom downstairs. Now, she pulled out the same paper and pointed to the forged room order. "Senora Franco's room."

The man's gaze slid suspiciously over Lara's bobbed wig and down her uniform. "Move aside."

"Si." Lara nodded, then said, "Okay?" as if she wasn't sure of the right answer. But the bodyguard had already shoved the shelf of cleaning supplies to one side of the cart and dug through the collection of dirty linen.

Finding nothing, he straightened. "Okay. Third door on the left."

"Gracias," Lara answered timidly, hurrying to push the bin down the corridor.

At the door, she paused, giving her heart a moment to slow down. "That was close."

"You bet it was," Ian agreed, the sarcasm palpable. "You know at least two other languages, but if I remember right, Spanish isn't one of them. If he'd known how to speak it, your cover would've been blown."

Lara had learned Russian over the past few years with Labyrinth and French—out of spite to her father—during high school and college. Her Spanish vocabulary was painfully limited, restricted to her secret passion for Spanish pop music.

"Well, he didn't know it, did he?" Lara quipped and opened the door. Since most of the hotel staff sported a Russian or French accent, she didn't want to chance either. When a language barrier existed, fewer questions were asked.

She maneuvered through the suite and into the bedroom. Normally, the maids wouldn't take the laundry bins into the room, but Lara had to risk it. The plastic had been removed, along with Sophia. Lara pushed the frustration away, but the sad ache remained.

"The guard is at his post." Ian advised. "It's now or never, Red."

LARA REACHED UNDERNEATH the bin, found the duct tape and ripped her small utility case free.

"First sign of trouble, I want you out of there."

Lara noticed that another door stood at the back of the suite. "I think I found the private entrance." With luck, Davidenko was asleep.

The hallway was small. Lara followed it until she reached the first door. Bedroom or office? She twisted the knob, found it open.

Quickly, she slipped inside. Closed curtains kept the room in darkness. Lara switched on her penlight. She hadn't the space in her small threefold case to bring her infrareds.

"I'm in Davidenko's suite." Lara moved, searching for another way. "It's his sitting room, not the office."

"Look for a connecting door."

"I am." On quiet feet, Lara crossed the room, found another entrance. "Found one locked." Quickly, Lara pulled Ian's cell phone from her pocket, placed it by the electronic keypad and punched the talk key. A low series of tones sounded. Within moments Lara heard a soft but audible click. "I'm in."

"Okay, you're doing fine. Our guy is still by the elevator."

Lara crossed to the desk, ignoring the monitors and sat in front of the computer. "Let's hope this works." She inserted the disk, then booted up the computer.

"You'll know in a second," Ian warned. "If it doesn't, I want you out of there five seconds after."

Lara didn't respond. Instead she watched while the program started running passwords through the computer. Thousands of words passed through. If Davidenko had used a combination number-letter password the program wouldn't work.

Minutes passed. Lara started opening drawers, searching for anything that might provide a clue to the password.

Suddenly, the screen blinked, then loaded. "No way. He used Moscow," she said shocked. "It worked, hotshot. I'm in."

"Okay, the information will be somewhere filed on his hard drive."

"Ian, I've got access to all his business. His accounts. His shipments. Even his payoffs," she noted. "Hell, it looks like he owns half the drug enforcement agency."

"That will take too long to download, Red. Stick to the plan."

"I'm not going to get another opportunity."

"Damn it. Find the formula first."

Lara ignored him and initiated the download of Davidenko's records.

"Our guy is on the move," Ian said, his voice low. "He's making rounds. Get the hell out of there."

"Hold on. I haven't found the *Katts Smeart* files," she whispered. Seconds ticked by, but Lara had lost all track of the time as she focused on the screen. Systematically she opened file after file. "It's not here, Ian. He must have it in a safe somewhere."

"Too late. Too late. Alexei's coming through the front in three…two…" Lara hit the computer shutdown, heard the whir of the hard drive snap off. She dropped to her knees and rolled under the desk.

The door clicked open. Slowly, she pulled the chair into the desk. A second later, light flooded the room.

Lara slid her hand up her thigh until she felt the warm metal of the switchblade she'd strapped there earlier.

Blood pounded in her ears. Slowly, she took a deep breath. If the guard came around the desk, she'd be cornered.

A bead of sweat rolled between her shoulder blades.

"Alexei!"

Lara stiffened at the shout from the guard's walkie-talkie.

"Yeah?" Alexei's voice rumbled above the desk.

Lara's breath backed up in her chest. Careful to make no noise, she released the blade from its sheath.

"Report to security. Someone shut down the surveillance system."

Ian, Lara thought.

"On my way."

She heard Alexei's footsteps retreat, then Ian's voice thundered in her ear.

"Get the hell out of there!"

"WHAT WERE YOU DOING?"

"My job, Ian. I have enough evidence to roast Davidenko, Anton Novak and half the government officials from coast to coast."

"I don't give a damn about them. Your job was to get the *Katts Smeart* files. Not to take chances with your life."

As it turned out, Lara's escape had been less complicated. After Alexei left, Lara double-checked the desk—fixing everything she'd disturbed before slipping out.

With Alexei gone, no one else appeared at the elevator. It had taken her less than an hour to lose the maid disguise and return to the hotel room.

"It's my life." Lara regarded him sharply, daring him to disagree. "But it's not me you're worried about, but the baby."

"You weren't thinking about the baby. Only getting the information."

"Trust me, Ian, I'm always thinking about this baby." Too restless to sit, she moved to the window.

A French countryside lay at her feet. Winding paths banked with a palette of pastel flora and foliage. Any other time, she would've enjoyed the view. Now it was just a grim reminder of what she couldn't have. "But that doesn't mean I've figured out what I'm going to do with it."

"It's not an *it,* Lara. It's a human being. A tiny life growing inside you. Most consider that a miracle, you know."

"No, anyone can have a baby. The miracle is in the parents. I can't even imagine where to begin raising a decent human being," Lara said. The admission hurting the deepest part of her heart. "Look at the two kids who tried to rob us earlier. They couldn't have been more than sixteen or seventeen."

"Lara, most kids turn out civilized, given the right guidance."

"That's easy for you to say, MacAlister. Your family is the damn Brady Bunch," Lara retorted, knowing her frustration stemmed from the fact that she'd fallen in love with him, long before. And everything that made him who he was.

His sense of family, his moral convictions. The backbone of integrity underlying both. His automatic acceptance of their child. The soft edge of his humanity.

Everything, Lara admitted, she wasn't.

"Your sister's a genius. Cain's the director of Labyrinth and head of MacAlister Securities, a Fortune 500 company. And his wife, Celeste, is a national hero." Lara waved her hand in the air. "And you, you..."

"I'm what?" His voice dipped into seductive mode.

What I can't have. "Never mind. I'm not in the mood to feed your ego."

Ian's lips twitched. He'd never seen Lara this unnerved. A sudden desire to protect her had him shifting closer. "We've had our problems."

"What? Chicken pox? Maybe an ingrown toenail or two?" She didn't try to hide the sarcasm.

"My dad wasn't born rich, Lara. And my mother worked hard to put herself through medical school."

"My point exactly. Look how much they've accomplished. Your mom is one of the finest plastic surgeons in the world. Not the country, but the world. And your dad runs his whiskey empire." She swung around from the window to face Ian. "One, I might add, he can't wait to pass on to you."

"Where did you hear that?"

"Kate told me about your passion for making whiskey." The fact was that Ian hadn't told her. She'd never experienced that much intimacy. The sharing of one's thoughts or feelings.

"Kate talks too much," Ian said dismissively. "I haven't decided anything yet."

But he would, Lara knew. She'd seen anticipation light his eyes at the mere mention of the possibility. The question was when. Tomorrow? Five years from now? "The bottom line is, you can't relate to what

I'm talking about. It's been ten years since I first met your parents and they haven't changed. You're lucky to be part of such a wonderful, loving family."

"Then give me the baby," he suggested, his tone hushed.

Pain sliced through her. She'd thought about it. A hundred times. But he was an operative right now. Could she trust him to walk away from it all? "Ian, you're in the same career…my dad—"

"Your dad's choice won't necessarily be mine. Besides, your dad loves you, Red."

"I know he does," Lara retorted. "But this isn't about love, Ian. This is about being there."

"He was a government agent. He couldn't risk your life."

"And what about my mother? The one I've never met?" She sank into a nearby chair and pulled her feet into a lotus position. "Her choice by the way."

"And so, you're going to prove them right, by doing the same thing? By walking away from the baby?"

"I understand better than anyone what my dad went through—what he gave up. He had no choice, but that doesn't make it any easier to accept."

Her voice wavered, and Ian understood. "You think you're too much like your father and mother to raise a child."

It was more than that. Lara wasn't idealistic, wasn't into sugarcoating the harsh realities of life. She met life on her terms, head-to-head. And she understood deep down, if this child was ever going to have a chance, it would be with another woman.

"Besides the fact that my maternal gene pool is nonexistent—I am my father's daughter. And being spies is what we do." There wasn't a note of apology in her tone. She'd made her decision long ago, and refused to offer excuses now. "And we do it better by not getting attached. Hell, my dad almost died two months ago and I was the last to know about it. Can't get more unattached than that."

"You were the last to know because we had to insure Jon's safety," Ian responded matter of fact.

Jon Mercer had been shot by an armed assassin who was after the President. For Jonathon's own protection, Cain chose at the time to let the world believe Jonathon had died, rather than reveal he'd slipped into a coma.

"I'm a trained government agent. I could've protected him. Instead, you kept me away from him. Lied to me about his condition. I won't have a child live that same life. Our life, Ian."

"I was under orders," Ian replied, surly.

"Orders. Did you sleep with me under orders? To keep me occupied?" Lara jumped up, paced. Dealing with her feelings for Ian wasn't something she faced sitting down.

"If I remember right, there was no sleeping involved."

Lara swung around. "For God's sake, you told me my father was dead!"

"He came pretty damn close."

"I don't know which was worse." She crossed her arms to keep from smacking him in the head. "The fact that you lied and let me grieve or the fact that you held me while I grieved."

"I saved your life. You would've gone off half-cocked—after the wrong person I might add—all in the name of vengeance. Cain knew it, I knew it." At the time, Lara had thought Cain's fiancée, Celeste, had killed Jonathon—part of a plot to assassinate the President—until the real killer had been identified.

"But my father didn't."

"He was in a coma. It wasn't his decision."

"We had sex, Ian. On the floor of the VI room. It wasn't romantic, it was a WWE takedown. I didn't expect undying love, but neither did I expect betrayal."

"The sex—as you so delicately put it—happened two weeks before your dad's shooting. So don't try and tell me that's the reason for all this contempt. No matter how it started—"

"It started over your choice of code names remember? And some stupid Greek mythology story." Her mind burned with the memory, the humiliation when she'd found out.

"Eos's lust over Orion was just a coincidence."

"Unrequited lust. She had the hots for him, but he could've cared less." She glared at him.

"Orion was a hunter." He glared back. "It seemed to fit—"

Lara snorted.

Ian met her eyes. "What we had was amazing, Red, but like you said, it was just sex—"

"I trusted you after that, damn it. And I don't trust anyone."

"Trusted me to do what? You're the one who laid down the rules that night. This is just casual, you said. Scratching an itch."

"God—" She looked up at the ceiling. "Why didn't we stop it?"

"Sweetheart, the moment I can stop spontaneous combustion, I'll retire a millionaire."

"You're already a millionaire," she snapped, not willing to give in to his charm. As one of the three heirs to the MacAlister fortune, Ian stood to inherit quite a lot more than a million dollars.

"That's beside the point."

"We agreed to keep it simple—no strings. I didn't expect…I didn't want to…" She struggled for the right word, knowing no word existed that wouldn't give him the wrong impression.

"To what?" He moved then, quick, quiet. Like a cat with a cornered mouse. Still, she didn't protest when his arms circled her, when his muscles—rock hard—tightened around her. With Ian came the warmth, the reassuring comfort.

Damn it, she wanted the comfort. Needed it.

But only from him.

She'd fought arms dealers, murderers, cartels.

Each made her stronger, more determined. Each took a piece of her soul. But whatever battle she'd fought in the past, none had taken more of a toll than fighting her love for Ian.

"To care about you. Okay? I didn't want to care about you." Suddenly, her stomach rolled. The tears pricked. "Are you happy?"

Ian's body tensed. "Lara—"

"Shut up, MacAlister. Your lies destroyed any feeling I might have had for you." She stepped out of his arms, dealt with the immediate sense of loss. Hoped her statement would come true soon enough. "So let's just get this over with, all right?"

Ian studied her for a moment, understanding a minefield when he saw one. Normally, he'd take the risk, but something held him back. The stubborn set of her jaw, the fear that threatened to crack the facade.

"All right." He sighed. "Let's get naked, then."

Chapter Eight

Thursday, 1400 hours

Getting naked, as Ian put it, meant going in without cover or backup. Literally, exposing themselves.

And for that reason, Lara had chosen schoolmarm sexy—draped in wealthy chic.

She wore a slightly off-the-shoulder dress, its sunshine yellow set fire to the honey highlights in her hair, the glint of satisfaction in her eyes.

"How am I doing?" she whispered, but the laughter was there, threatening to bubble forward. The loose cotton skimmed her body, catching provocatively on the soft curves beneath. With each long-legged step, Lara drew more than one appreciative male glance. Ian ignored them all until a soft wolf whistle reached them from the other side of the lobby.

Ian ground his back teeth. "You're doing just fine." He grabbed her elbow, staking his claim.

"Can I help you?" A young woman, with chunky

streaks of blond hair and a California tan, greeted them from behind the registration desk.

Ian's frown gave way to a slow, sexy smile. "I hope so," he drawled, his eyes dipped to her name tag. "Mrs.—"

"Miss," the woman interjected, almost too hurriedly. "Miss Amoretti." Her gaze lingered over his designer white T-shirt that hugged and defined, before drifting to the vintage jeans, factory scarred and faded, that rode low on lean hips.

Ian's smile widened all the way to his wisdom teeth. Amazed, Lara could do no more than just stand there and observe. After all, the man was a champ when it came to manipulating women.

"Well, Miss Amoretti, my name is Ian MacAlister." He leaned forward, placing a forearm onto the counter, then dropped his voice to a conspiratorial whisper. "And this is Lara Mercer."

The young woman blinked, then her toffee-brown eyes widened with recognition.

"Hello, Miss Mercer."

"Hello," Lara responded, noting Miss Amoretti's gaze rested a polite three seconds on Lara before darting back to Ian. "What can I do for you today?"

"We would like your best suite," he said, then winked.

"A suite," Miss Amoretti repeated, her expression dazed.

Lara coughed, covering a snort of disgust.

Ian shot her a two-second don't-you-dare-blow-this glare, before turning back to Miss Amoretti. "The best suite you have."

The loss of eye contact with Ian must have brought the California girl to her senses. "Mr. MacAlister, I wish I could, but unfortunately, we don't have a reservation—"

"Don't believe in them," he interrupted easily, ignoring the fact that Lara's eyebrow arched. "You see, Miss Mercer and I woke up this morning feeling lucky and want to take it out for a spin at your baccarat tables."

"You woke up…I—I see." The young woman glanced at Lara, who batted her eyes. "That's wonderful," she said, her cheeks flushed. "I mean it's wonderful that you thought of the Bontecou. Still, I don't see any way we can accommodate you today. Maybe—"

"Can I be of assistance?" A frail, but cultured voice drifted from behind Lara. Before she could turn around, a little man, no older than fifty, appeared at her elbow.

"Monsieur, mademoiselle," he greeted them, then bowed his head with an exaggerated pause. "My name is Bernard. I am the manager of Château Bontecou."

"It's nice to meet you," Lara responded and extended her hand. She noted the man's pointed chin, high cheekbones and perfectly thin, straight nose and decided Bernard had formed an intimate relationship with a cosmetic surgeon.

"Thank you." The older man attempted to shake her hand, but abandoned the gesture after a brief, limp-wristed squeeze of her fingers.

"I couldn't help but hear your request, Mr. MacAlister. Of course, we'll accommodate you."

Apparently the MacAlister name entitled Ian to preferential treatment, Lara thought wryly.

"I insist you stay in the Presidential Penthouse suite at no charge." He glanced at Miss Amoretti. "Take care of it, Maria."

"Yes, sir," Maria answered, relief infusing each word. Quickly, she started typing at the computer behind the desk.

"Thank you for all your help, Miss Amoretti." Ian winked at Maria, easing the tense edges of her smile.

"You understand, Bernard," Lara said, careful to find the correct balance of charm—somewhere between Southern friendly and New York haughty. "Mr. MacAlister and I tend to draw crowds. Crowds that own cameras. And although I'm always in favor of free publicity for my father, we'd prefer to have a private few days to ourselves."

"Understood. I will personally guarantee your privacy," Bernard promised. "May I inform Mr. Davidenko of your arrival? He likes to know about his more...significant guests."

"By all means," Lara answered appreciatively.

"One last favor." Ian set his leather briefcase on the counter. "I have something for your hotel safe. If you have the space."

Bernard laughed. "Oh, we have space, Mr. MacAlister. We have plenty of space."

WITH PATIENCE CAME POWER. And Mikhail Davidenko was a very patient man.

He leaned back in his leather chair, observed the bank of monitors and considered the events of the last forty-eight hours.

The missing *Katts Smeart,* the munitions and million dollars were obvious losses, but none he couldn't recoup. Even if the *Katts Smeart* hit the population, the demonstration of its potential power would boost the agent's market price.

And when Anton replaced the military cache and money, Mikhail's loss would be minimal.

No, there were other concerns. The first, retrieving the missing *Katts Smeart* files.

And of course, Anton's failure. Disappointing after twenty-five years.

And now, according to his hotel manager, Ian MacAlister and Lara Mercer had shown up at his doorstep—on a whim.

The first two might be a coincidence. But the last?

Mikhail had never dealt personally with the MacAlisters—had known about Quentin and his wife, Christel, by reputation only. Same with Vice President Jonathon Mercer.

Mikhail harbored no illusion as to why.

The MacAlisters and Mercers were formidable apart. But together they were impenetrable.

His business worked better with those he could manipulate through vices—preferably drugs, sex, greed or revenge. Neither they, nor their offspring, weakened to vices. They harbored no skeletons. They stood by their principles, held no patience with compromises—political or otherwise. And had a tight, influential circle of associates and friends to back them up.

Until today. When a whim placed two members within his reach. Mikhail let out a small, derisive laugh. Not likely.

On the monitors, he could see the couple being escorted into their room. Their arms looped around each other, the familiarity of Ian's hand on the woman's back, the smile of adoration from her—all reinforced an appearance of intimacy, maybe even love.

Mikhail never based any opinion on appearance alone.

A lesson he'd learned years ago.

In his youth, Mikhail had observed his father, a Russian Mafia leader, during a weekly poker game. The elder Davidenko was passionate about the game.

On this particular night, his father had folded,

conceded the hand—and the large pot of money—to his top enforcer, Marco.

Smiling, Marco raked in his winnings, but not before he boasted to his Mafia boss that he'd bluffed him with a seven-four off suit.

Mikhail's father laughed, then slapped Marco good-naturedly on the back. After all, the two men had been comrades for over ten years.

Moments later, Mikhail's father had pulled out his pistol, stuck the barrel in Marco's gut and pulled the trigger.

The enforcer fell to the floor, dead.

Later, when Mikhail asked his father why he killed the man, his father smiled and said, "The poker table is business—not games. You want a man's secrets? Play poker with him."

"And Marco?" Mikhail had asked.

"He lied too well."

It was a lesson Mikhail had never forgotten.

Suddenly, his private line buzzed, forcing his thoughts back to the present. "Yes, what is it, Joseph?"

"I have the information on this morning's mishap, Mr. Davidenko."

"You mean the camera system," Mikhail affirmed, mentally adding the glitch to his list.

Joseph entered the office and closed the door. He approached Davidenko's desk. "An outside source interfered with the camera link."

"Have you found this source?"

"No. But we will. It's just a matter of time," Joseph answered. "The device used had to be sophisticated enough to bypass our security traps. Only an expert on securities could've pulled it off, Mr. Davidenko."

"I agree. Our system is too advanced for an amateur." Davidenko folded his hands, then tapped his lips with his finger. He glanced at the couple on the monitor. It was a well-known fact that Cain, the oldest MacAlister brother, ran an international security company and had developed most of the government's security programs. Another coincidence?

Mikhail rose from his chair. "Joseph, I need you to arrange an extra seat at the poker table tomorrow." Mikhail walked over to the five-hundred-gallon fish tank. Gently he tapped the glass, amused when his beauties scattered. Some hid in an assortment of plants, while most darted behind various pieces of driftwood and rocks strewn on the bottom. "I want to invite a very important guest." With a turn of a knob, he dimmed the tank's light. Several came out of hiding, their red bellies sleek, almost incandescent.

"Yes, sir." But the surprise was there, deep in the gray eyes. Ever since Anton had become Davidenko's man, he'd arranged the weekly poker nights.

The man had been Mikhail's enforcer too long to question his orders. Mikhail reached under the counter and brought out a container of raw meat. He picked out a piece, feeling the stickiness of its still-fresh blood, catching the thick metallic scent of death in the air. "Did Alexei dispose of Miss Franco's remains?"

"Yes, sir."

"Good."

"Is that all, Mr. Davidenko?"

During his service, Joseph had declined several offers to become more involved in Davidenko's many interests, claimed he enjoyed his position and had no desire to change it.

Mikhail smiled, but his eyes remained on the piranha. "No, I need you to do me one more favor."

Joseph simply stood and waited. Mikhail stirred the water with practiced ease, getting his pets' attention. Methodically he dropped in the chunks of flesh and meat.

"I want you to keep a personal eye on Anton for the next few days. Without his knowing, of course. Alexei can fill in for you here," Mikhail ordered.

Always sensing the distrust between Joseph and Anton, Mikhail had never pushed the issue—simply because he enjoyed keeping both men where they served him best. Now, he suspected, circumstances had changed.

"Check in with me every hour, Joseph. Anton might be flexing his muscles, wanting a little independence." Mikhail tossed in the last of the piranhas' dinner. "If he is, I want to know if I should be...concerned."

Chapter Nine

Lara ran a hand over one of the twin Louis XV chairs, admiring the silver-white brocade, the heavily carved walnut frame.

Davidenko spared no expense on the decor.

The grand salon boasted of coffered ceilings with custom-made rock crystal chandeliers and an 180 degree view of Las Vegas. Each window stretched from floor to ceiling, their large frames swathed in plum silk drapes. Dark walnut furnishings, with cornflower-blue and eggshell brocade, appeared evenly balanced throughout the living area—all complementing the floor's checkered granite, sporadic tapestry hangings and a carved walnut fireplace.

The French certainly had a way of making one feel like royalty, she mused. "This is marvelous, darling."

Every room was monitored by camera and mike. Only the patio and the steam shower were clear.

Lara's heart sank. She'd have to keep up the charade indefinitely.

Ian stepped behind her and drew her against his chest. "You're welcome."

She leaned back, settled her head against his shoulder, heard his heart pounding beneath her ear. Without thinking, she let the comforting rhythm soothe her nerves.

Ian slipped his hand over her belly.

Her breath caught, hallowing the curve beneath his fingers. "Don't," she rasped. Forcing a smile, she stepped away.

"Look at the view." She opened the patio door.

When he followed her out, she turned on him. "Don't do that again, Ian," she snapped.

Ian grabbed her arm, pulled her against him. "It was either that or reach for your breast. Which would you prefer?"

"Neither."

"Lara, are you sure you're up for this?"

"Yes," Lara answered, her voice low. She decided not to yank away from his hold. "Just because I don't want to be groped—"

"It's all part of the illusion," Ian warned. "If Davidenko even suspects we're here for anything but a little gambling and some privacy, we're dead."

"The money helped." Lara rubbed her temple, trying to ease the tension. Lord, she was tired.

"Putting a million dollars into the safe might get his attention, but it won't get us where we need to be."

"Which is a private invite," Lara agreed. "And that still won't guarantee Novak."

"You realize if your priest is here, he's aware you and I are together."

"Either way, we're going to have to risk it," Lara said. "We're down to twenty-four hours, Ian. We can't—"

A knock at the door stopped Lara's reply. Ian loosened his hold and they both reentered the suite. With a simple nod in her direction, Ian opened the door.

A hotel employee stood in the doorway with a cart in front of him. "I have champagne and caviar. Compliments of Mr. Davidenko. May I come in, sir?"

"By all means." Ian's smile didn't quite reach his eyes.

The servant placed the tray and bucket on the nearby coffee table. "Mr. Davidenko is hosting a small cocktail party tonight in his suite. If possible, he would like you and Miss Mercer to come." The man opened the champagne. A pop exploded in the room. "Eight o'clock."

"Tell him we would be delighted," Lara said with a smile. "Won't we, darling?"

"Absolutely," Ian agreed.

"Very good, madam, monsieur." The man nodded. "My name is François. Should you need anything during your stay, just press the number one on your telephone. That is my direct line."

Lara picked up a flute of champagne in a subtle salute. "*Merci,* François."

"*Vous êtes bienvenue.* You are welcome, mademoiselle."

Lara took a small taste of champagne fizz while Ian closed the door behind François.

"Well, what a nice surprise," Lara purred and glanced at the bottle's label. "I like a man who has excellent taste in champagne."

Ian plucked the glass from her hand.

"What did you do that for?"

"No alcohol. You know how it upsets your stomach, honey."

"I wasn't drinking it, I was just holding it." Lara's chin tilted up, but she forced herself to laugh. "I love that you're so protective, but really, one sip wouldn't have hurt."

"You never know."

Lara bit back her scream of frustration. "So what should we do first?"

"Eat."

Lara grabbed the tray of beluga caviar and crackers. "Let's go out to the living room and enjoy the view."

Ian glanced at the terrace and frowned. But since she'd already started toward the room, she'd left him little choice but to follow.

Once they settled next to each other on the couch, Lara fed Ian a cracker with caviar on it.

After watching him chew for a moment, she helped herself to one. She hadn't realized how long it had been since she'd eaten. Still, the caviar could've been sand, for all it appealed to her.

"Darling, why don't you turn on the television? I want to see what my father's been up to lately."

Ian took the remote from the coffee table, turned to the local news and then he increased the volume, giving them a little privacy.

Ian tugged Lara toward him until she sat on his lap. Gently, he eased her head onto his shoulder, then settled back into the couch.

"Is this all necessary?" she whispered. "I figure an hour max and we can leave."

"If we're going to do this, I want to be comfortable," he murmured, enjoying the fact that she wasn't sniping. His fingers massaged the back of her neck. "Rest. Give your body a chance to recover. You've been up thirty-six hours, it's okay to take a catnap."

The exhaustion crept up on her, taking advantage of her relaxing muscles. "We should be downstairs tailing Novak," she grumbled halfheartedly and rubbed the grit from her eyes.

"Not for a while. They'll become suspicious if we keep disappearing on them. I've got the monitor here. I can keep an eye on Novak, Davidenko and their goons. After we've given Davidenko time to size us up, we'll slip out to the casino. I want to get a read on Novak, follow him a bit. If we're going to deliver him to the priest, we need to know the best way to get past his security."

Muscles loosened beneath his touch. Lara kicked off her shoes, brought her knees up until she curled in his lap.

"Ian?" She yawned against his neck. He smiled against her temple, fascinated by this softer Lara. "You never once asked me to prove the baby is yours."

"I know the baby is mine."

"How?"

Ian paused, deciding she deserved honesty. "Because what happened between us, wasn't ordinary, Red. It's taken me two months to come to terms with it. And I know you still haven't. But you will. You're a lot of things—stubborn Irish, for one—but you're not casual."

"You believe that?"

"Yes, I do." Something in his voice—the hard edge, the depth of conviction—must have convinced her that he was telling her the truth.

"I don't know what to say. I never—" She stopped when Ian heard the tears back up in her throat.

Slowly, she took his hand, then placed it on her stomach. "I guess we'll figure this one out together. Right, Dad?"

"Right." Emotions, too many to identify, rolled through Ian, caused his fingers to flex in response. With his free hand, he caressed Lara's hair, stroking the waves that spilled over his chest. He felt her eyes flutter shut, and within a few minutes, her breathing dipped into a soft cadence.

Come hell or Irish temper, he would protect his family.

THE SUN BEAT DOWN on the Hummer, its wrath unmerciful as it drove the temperature inside well over a hundred degrees.

Running the air conditioner was out of the question. Drew too much attention. Ian settled for the tufts of breeze and exhaust fumes that crossed through the open windows of the Hummer.

He'd opted for the outside using Davidenko's cameras, rather than firsthand contact. If Novak made a move, it would be off-site, away from Davidenko's spies.

Ian wanted a car ready and waiting.

His eyes slid to the dashboard clock, noted that Lara had been sleeping more than three hours. Out cold, she hadn't even twitched when he'd moved her from the couch to the bed.

At the time, he'd thought briefly about arranging a wake-up call, then immediately dismissed the idea. Tailing a suspect didn't take two people.

He glanced at the handheld computer, saw Novak hadn't left his desk. Ian's lips tilted with irony. Arms dealing generated a lot of paperwork.

Of course, he'd deal with Lara's fury later and

deep down he looked forward to it. Damned if Lara wasn't at her best in the midst of a temper tantrum.

That one time in the VI room, he'd harnessed all that flash and sass under him—and she launched him to the stars. Left him craving a lifetime of more.

But first, Ian thought, he'd take care of her problem. He shifted, swallowed some tepid water—used both to ease the desire. Novak left his office.

While he watched, Novak took the private elevator to the first floor, got off and crossed to the lobby.

"This is it," Ian said to himself. Straightening, he started the car and waited. It didn't take long.

He picked up Novak just as the arms dealer slid into a dark green Mercedes.

Ian shoved the Hummer into drive and followed the Mercedes down the drive and out onto the main strip.

Without warning, another Mercedes, a tan sedan, cut Ian off and jockeyed for a position behind Novak. Well, well. Another tail?

Ian dropped a car or two behind, making sure he kept both Mercedes sedans in view.

Another player? A partner maybe. Ian shifted in his seat, irritated. What the hell had Lara gotten herself into?

Both cars braked for a red light. Ian followed suit, his fingers tapping out his frustration on the wheel. If he got them out of this alive, he'd wring her stubborn neck.

Lara had been wrong, accusing him of putting

duty above all else. Hell, she couldn't have been more wrong. It hadn't been duty that had kept Ian by her side during her father's shooting, it had been personal.

Ian tapped the brake, allowed a sporty, red convertible to ease in front of him. It hadn't been the call of duty that motivated his retirement from the SEALs or his contract with Labyrinth. It had been personal. Lara had been personal. Once she joined the agency, there'd been no choice.

By the time Novak pulled up to a church, Ian had recognized the street. His little voice started working overtime.

"I'll be damned." He glanced at the sign. *St. Stanislaus Catholic Church.* Hell, it's just getting better and better, now isn't it?

He parked a half block from the tan sedan, keeping it between the Hummer and Novak. Content, he shut off the engine and waited—allowing the story to unfold.

A man, dressed in a black suit, got out of the tan Mercedes and moved to the sidewalk.

Davidenko's man.

While Ian watched, the suit leaned a hip against the car, crossed his arms and waited—making no secret of the fact he was watching the church.

Impatience itched at Ian's spine, but he knew better than to give in to it. Time slowed to a turtle's pace. Ten, then fifteen minutes passed.

Ian ground a cuss word between his back teeth. Novak returned with Father Xavier by his side. Somehow the arms dealer must have found out about the priest.

Instinctively, Ian reached for his gun and the car handle, then froze midmotion.

Novak opened the passenger door, took the priest's arm and helped him into the car. No force. No angry movement. Ian leaned back into his seat, his mind racing through different scenerios.

When Novak pulled from the curb, Davidenko's man followed.

Ian eased into traffic, then picked up his cell phone and hit the automatic dial.

Guilt hummed across the lines of his shoulders, but he pushed it back.

"MacAlister." Cain's voice sounded gritty, tired.

"Cain, it's Ian."

"What the hell happened to you? Why haven't you answered the phone?"

"I shut it off," Ian said, making no excuses, offering no apologies.

"Where are you?"

"In Vegas," Ian responded grimly. "We have a situation."

Thursday, 1600 hours

MACHINES LINED THE FLOOR, like tin soldiers, all in uniformed rows. Short, fat, tall, skinny. Most spewing noises of bells or old game shows. Others, the older ones spattered with color, were content to flash yellow strobes when someone hit the jackpot.

All were being tended to, their bellies fed with coins from eager hands holding little white buckets or cold, hard cash.

Lara found herself fitting in the former. She fed three five-dollar coins into an older slot machine that boasted patriotic stars of red, white and blue. Liking the irony, she'd chosen it on purpose. It had taken her less than an hour to lose four of her five hundred dollars. Less than that to work off her irritation with Ian.

Lara jabbed the Bet Max button.

The clock had showed just past three in the afternoon when she'd awakened. A quick search of the suite told her Ian had left. On the coffee table she found an apple and a note with one word on it. "Eat."

Underneath the note she found the key to Father Xavier's room. She pocketed the key and ate the apple.

Ian should have woken her up, but even she had to admit the sleep had done her good. The headache had gone, her eyes no longer burned. She'd lost three hours, but balanced against the exhaustion, she figured she was no worse off than before.

When the slot machine took her last fifteen dollars, Lara glanced at her watch. She couldn't waste another moment, stalling for Ian. Ian had taken the monitor, leaving little doubt that he'd followed Novak. A call to the valet station told her he'd taken the car.

Slowly, she wandered over to the public restroom. Inside, she made her way to an empty stall.

When a little girl suddenly stepped in her path, Lara shifted and grabbed the sink's counter.

The girl, dressed in pink shorts and a top with a big dinosaur on it, pointed at Lara's hair. The slant of her hazel eyes widened with wonder. "Pretty."

"Hello." Enamored, Lara crouched and touched the little girl's straight black hair, tickled her cheek with an errant lock. "Pretty."

The little girl blinked, then laughed and clapped her hands.

"Jenny?"

Lara glanced over her shoulder and saw the mother.

Her Asian heritage defined her features. The exotic slant of her cheeks, the oval face. The thick curtain of hair caught back in a band and black as pitch. All framed a pair of almond eyes and perfectly arched brows.

"Jenny?" The mother glanced around.

Lara stepped back, giving the woman a clean line of sight. "She's right here."

"Jenny," she said with relief. "I asked you to stand right by my leg, sweetie."

Jenny, who couldn't have been more than three, smiled. "Pretty." Again the little girl pointed at Lara.

"Yes, she is." A smile touched the woman's lips. "Very pretty, but next time, stay close. Okay?"

"Okay."

Jenny's mother lifted a baby from the changing table—a boy with fuzzy porcupine hair and chubby cheeks—and settled him onto her hip. Lara put the other woman's age close to her own age of thirty.

"They're adorable," Lara commented softly and gave in to the urge to caress Jenny's cheek.

"Thank you," the woman said, her jade eyes sharpened with interest. "Having two is a handful, but I wouldn't trade it for anything." The woman studied Lara, caught something in her expression. "Do you have any children?"

Lara smiled, felt the familiar prick at her eyes. "I'm two months pregnant with my first."

"Congratulations." The woman's smile increased before she noticed the hint of tears. "Dealing with those hormones, huh?"

Lara blinked. "Oh yeah."

"And morning sickness?"

"No, just bouts of nausea."

"Onions?"

"Red meat." Lara laughed. God, it felt so good to share with someone who understood. "So far."

"Well, don't let that or anyone spoil these next few months. Kids don't start being your kids once they're born." She patted her stomach. "They start being yours in here."

"I guess they do."

"You're the first person that's going to know your baby. No one else will feel it grow or—" she chuckled "—hiccup. Once they're born, each stage is wonderful, but they grow so fast." The woman sighed and nuzzled her son's cheek. "Whatever you do, don't listen to women's delivery stories and rough pregnancies. Just enjoy."

"Thanks, I'll remember that." Lara smiled.

"Listen to me, I should take my own advice and leave you alone," she remarked. "Even without it, you'll be a good mom."

"How can you be so sure?" Lara asked, curious. Not because she wanted the compliment. She truly wanted to know why another mother would think so.

The woman glanced at her daughter. "Intuition." Then she held out her hand. "Good luck with your baby, Miss Mercer."

Lara stiffened, for a moment forgetting she was recognizable. "I—"

She winked. "Don't worry, your secret's safe with me." She opened the door. "And watch out for that red meat."

"I will," Lara said, then wiggled her fingers goodbye to Jenny.

Slowly, Lara entered the stall, stripped off her sundress splashed with red roses and leaves. Underneath she wore white shorts. From her purse she pulled out a white halter and slipped it on.

For the first time, Lara contemplated a life with a child. The emotion, the responsibility. In all her adult years, she'd never acknowledged the possibility. Never let herself dwell on the thought of marriage and family. But now, the longing for both tugged at her.

Several voices boomed in the restroom, startling her. Quickly, she tucked her hair into the nylon cap and put on her black wig. Adjusting it into place, she slipped on her sunglasses and waited until there was a rush at the vanity, then she left the stall. She washed her hands, finger smoothed her hair in the mirror, then followed the larger part of the crowd out the door.

Keeping with the group, Lara entered the fullest elevator. Her? A mother? The elevator slid open at her floor and she stepped off.

Lara thought of Jenny and the baby as she walked down the hall. Something had happened to her when she'd touched the little girl. A surge of power shifted in her, lessening the fear of the unknown.

Lara slid the key into the lock and twisted the handle. Before she could react, the door opened, a vise clamped on to her wrist and yanked her in.

Chapter Ten

Lara threw her weight into her assailant, then swung her fist.

"Damn it, Red." Ian caught her punch with his free hand. "Don't you ever look before you swing?"

"Not when I'm grabbed." She shook off his hand and shoved him aside. "What's up with the caveman routine?"

"That." Ian nodded toward the floor.

Father Xavier Varvarinski lay dead, his eyes open, half his jaw and skull gone.

"Don't touch anything," Ian said, his voice grim. "I've already cleaned the room of our fingerprints."

Lara noted the gun next to Father Xavier's hand. "Whoever did this wants the authorities to think it's a suicide." Fear rifled through her. With Father Xavier gone, she had no way of getting the antibiotic. Not without help.

"Ian, we've got a bigger problem," Lara murmured, catching the tinny scent of old blood, the thicker scent of urine. Acid crept to the back of her throat. She blew out a breath, swallowed it back. Damn it, this wasn't her first dead body.

"Father Xavier told me he'd contaminated his rosary with the *Katts Smeart.*" Her eyes locked with Ian's. "After he'd given it to me."

"His rosary…" Ian's jaw flexed. "You're infected."

"Actually, I'm not sure." Only tight control kept her voice calm, the waver whisper thin. She reached into her purse for a mint. Ignored the tremble in her fingers when she brought it to her mouth. "Father Xavier planted the cross in the confessional. When he'd told me he had something for me, I naturally assumed it was the *Katts Smeart*. Turns out, I'd picked up the rosary. Five minutes later, he told me he dipped the cross in the chemical agent."

"But you have no proof."

She shook her head. "After he left, I took care not to touch anything. I washed the cross and its box in the church bathroom. If he had contaminated the rosary, I couldn't risk exposing anyone else."

"You should've risked it, damn it. You should have found out for sure."

"How? Fly all the back to Norfolk, drop off the rosary and then travel back to Las Vegas before the arms deal last night? Even if the margin of time was big enough, if I brought anyone else into this, he threatened to release the agent," she reminded him.

"Lara—"

"I'm sorry, Ian. Maybe I should've told you sooner—"

"Maybe?" he snarled. "And the body? Is the baby infected?"

"The baby's fine," Lara answered, pushing her own fears away. Antagonism sizzled the air. Enough to raise Lara's defenses. "Telling you now doesn't change the timeline or the urgency behind finding the poison. If Novak was working with Father Xavier, he still could release that agent on hundreds of unsuspecting people."

"We don't need to locate him. He brought the priest here."

Lara swung around, her eyes intense. "What?"

"While you were sleeping, I tracked Novak to Saint Stan's. He picked up Father Xavier. I lost them here at the hotel. Actually, I lost the monitored transmission."

"A malfunction?"

"Maybe," Ian replied, but his tone indicated otherwise. "When I opened the door, I found the priest dead."

Lara paced, her mind running through the possibilities. "They've been in this together."

"And unless I miss my guess," Ian agreed, "Father Xavier blew up the trailer and killed the other arms dealer, Armand."

"How do you figure?" Lara tried to picture the frail priest holding a rocket launcher. "He didn't have enough strength."

Ian turned over the older man's hands. "Flash burns."

"Did you search him?"

"Yes, he's clean. Except for this." Ian handed her an old leather Bible.

"This is too worn to be from the room." Lara opened it, caught the musty scent of incense. Her eyes glimpsed some handwriting on the inside page. "To my beloved Xavier. Yours always, Katia."

"Too personal for a sister." Lara flipped through the pages. Found nothing. "An old girlfriend?" She hesitated then slipped the book in her purse.

"Okay. So if Father Xavier and Novak were working together, why kill the priest now?"

"They'd drawn suspicion. I spied one of Davidenko's men tailing Novak."

"Which one?" Lara asked. "Alexei?"

"No. One I haven't seen, but he's definitely with Davidenko."

"How can you be sure?"

"The suit. All Davidenko's goons are wearing them. Russian tailored. Butch-black. No taste. Pricey."

Lara nodded, then stopped. "Davidenko's man could've killed Father Xavier, too." Lara's head shot up. "The cameras."

"Whoever shot him has access to the security cameras. I'll bet you that briefcase of money, any disks have been wiped clean."

"We could always grab Novak and pound the information out of him."

"That wouldn't do any good."

"It would make me feel better."

Ian raised his eyebrow. "Getting a little blood-thirsty?"

Lara's stomach flopped. "Please don't mention blood and thirsty together. Not right now."

"Sorry." The concern was there, in the slant of his brow.

Suddenly uneasy, Lara studied the body. "You realize we need to leave him here."

"For now. Blowing the whistle would bring in too many Domestics." Domestic was the agency term for police and Bureau boys. "If we bring anyone in, it's going to be Cain."

"No."

"I said *if*," Ian snapped.

Lara dismissed the censure. "The antidote is gone."

"Maybe," Ian agreed slowly, his gaze taking in ruffled bedcovers, the slightly open drawers. "Whoever killed the priest searched the room. Unless the *Katts Smeart* and files were on Father Xavier at the time, the killer didn't find anything. The room was clean, I searched it earlier."

"So," Lara commented. "We go to Davidenko's party."

"If they were partners, Novak might have the agent and the antidote. Or at least one of the two. Could be he killed Father Xavier for it." Ian glanced down at the priest. "Either way, we can get a read on Novak there."

"If he *is* there."

"Novak is Davidenko's right-hand man." Ian's eyes narrowed. "He'll be there. Unless he's dead, too."

LARA STOPPED and stood in front of the entry's gilded mirror. Her gaze skimmed critically over the midthigh, silk slip dress. Small black beads trimmed the bodice, clinging to the roundness of her breasts. The tanzanite silk molded to her curves, emphasized the flat of her stomach, her slim hips. She turned and peered over her shoulder in the mirror. The dress, backless, dipped into a low swoop across the base of her spine.

Perfect.

Her looks were the one thing she could thank her mother for. The only thing.

The product of an affair with a French countess, Lara had never doubted her father's sense of responsibility or her mother's disdain.

Up until age six, she'd been cared for by a series of nannies. After, she'd been shipped off to her first boarding school not knowing at the time she wouldn't return home again until she was eighteen. At first, her father had tried to write sporadic letters, bring her home for the occasional holiday. Each letter had been signed with his name, Jonathon, and each she was sure, penned by his secretary. As for the holidays, the first few visits home, he'd been away on assignment.

Within a few years, the period between letters stretched longer, then eventually became nonexistent.

So had her homecomings.

Lara shifted, satisfied when the beads blinked, drawing the eye. She'd learned long ago that appearance was ninety percent of the game.

Appear to be a family. Appear to be happy. Appear to be in control.

She'd pulled back her hair into a loose bun that allowed wisps of hair to soften the outer edge of her face, draw a male gaze to the graceful line of her neck.

"Are you ready?" Ian asked from behind, catching her reflection in the mirror, noting how it accented Lara's fragility, her beauty. His eyes flickered over her. Her breasts were a little fuller, he noted. In his mind's eye, he pictured her belly, round and heavy with the baby, adding a tantalizing curve to the cascade of silk. How the delicate material stretched softly against her with each step.

"One second." She turned away to grab her small black clutch from a Louis XV dresser and in doing so, gave Ian the full view of her naked back.

"Go change." The words were low, but threatening.

"Why?" She checked herself with a long, practiced gaze—giving him another glimpse of her bare back, the silk across the swell of her bottom. "What's wrong?"

"Damn it, Lara. How in the hell are you wearing anything beneath?"

"Ian," Lara purred, but there was steel underlining his name. "This is perfectly acceptable for a cocktail party, darling." The game had shifted, time was running out.

"What? To wear clothes that leave nothing to the imagination?"

"Now, you're sounding like a jealous lover." She sauntered over to him, leaned in until they were only a breath apart. "Besides, the only thing I'm wearing *is* the dress…." She took his hand and slid it high up her thigh. Felt the calluses rough against her skin. Enjoyed the shiver his touch brought. His fingers caught on the thin Velcro strap, then shifted, sliding inside her thigh until they touched the cold steel of the switchblade. "And this."

"MISS MERCER?"

Lara swung around and caught the appreciative, but icy glint in Mikhail Davidenko's gaze.

"Hello, Mr. Davidenko. It's nice to finally meet you." She offered her hand.

"If I'd known it would be such a pleasant experience, Miss Mercer, I would've arranged it years ago." Slowly, he brought her hand up to his lips, his dark eyes never wavering from hers.

His mouth brushed her skin, his lips reptile cold. Lara forced a smile and let her hand drop from his.

"So what brings you both to my hotel?"

"A little time to ourselves," Lara said, her gaze

skimming his suite, taking in the opulent decor. "We've heard you take pride in maintaining a certain elegant standard and level of privacy for your guests."

"Absolutely. I hope we've met your expectations so far."

"So far," Lara answered with dry amusement.

Novak stepped behind Davidenko, whispered a short comment in his ear. Davidenko nodded. "May I introduce you to my associate? Anton Novak."

"Mr. Novak." This time, Lara didn't offer her hand.

"Miss Mercer."

"Anton is in charge of my import and export business," Mikhail commented. "As I get older, I find I have no interest in the day-to-day corporate world and prefer to spend more of my time here, with my guests."

"I can see why. It's very beautiful."

"It's been my experience that true beauty recognizes true beauty," Mikhail murmured.

"I'm flattered—"

"I hope I'm not interrupting…." Ian's voice indicated otherwise. Her gaze snapped to Ian, but he'd been expecting it and met the flash of temper with a raised eyebrow. Maybe it was pride, or even impatience, but she'd remember he was in the room, by God.

Deliberately his hand slid across the base of her spine. His fingers dipped possessively below the material, felt the shiver up her spine.

"No, our host was just telling me about his hotel," Lara said smoothly. "Mikhail Davidenko, this is my…friend, Ian MacAlister."

Both men shook hands.

"And this is his associate Mr. Novak, Ian. You both have something in common. He deals with Mikhail's export business. I'm sure since you've been helping your father, you must have come across each other."

"Can't say that I have."

Mikhail's eyes hadn't moved from Lara. "Miss Mercer was just telling me how you came to stay at the Bontecou. I'm very pleased you trust me. With your privacy, that is." He laughed.

"So far we haven't been disappointed. Have we, darling?" Ian said before tipping his glass toward Novak. "What do you export, Novak?"

"This and that. Mostly tech. Less gamble, more profit."

"You don't like to gamble?" Ian's eyes met Novak's. The steel in them parried, then thrust. "Considering where we're standing that's hard to believe."

"Mr. Davidenko is the gambler here."

"In fact, MacAlister, I'm having a private game tomorrow around noon. Texas Holdem. Cash only. You're more than welcome to join myself and a few of my—" Mikhail winked at Lara "—friends."

In that instant, Lara glimpsed the charm beneath and understood how Sophia had a hard time resisting.

"Some will be flying in later tonight, others early tomorrow."

"I've heard of Five and Seven card stud," Lara commented. "What is Texas Holdem?"

"It's a variation on Seven Card stud," Mikhail replied. "I prefer it. Most do, if you follow the poker tournaments these days. All seem to be Texas Holdem games."

"And the difference?" Lara asked.

"Initially, two cards are dealt facedown to each player, then there is a betting round. Three cards, customarily called the flop, are then dealt faceup in the center of the table. Those three community cards are part of each player's hand. The players have another opportunity to bet."

"Another card is dealt in the center, followed by another betting round," Ian inserted. "Then a final card is dealt—also in the center."

"If you're still in the game, you have another chance to bet. The winner is determined by the highest five-card hand."

"Doesn't sound too hard." Lara's lips dipped into a perfect rich girl's pout. "Are women allowed?"

"No, unfortunately they are not. You see, my friends are very old and set in their Russian ways."

"What are the stakes?" Ian asked, making note that Mikhail's friends were also Russian.

"Minimum two hundred thousand, but most keep one million on hand."

"No problem. It just so happens I have one million sitting in your safe downstairs," Ian said easily. "Or maybe you knew that?"

"Maybe I did." Mikhail laughed. "You'd be surprised at what I know, I think."

LARA STALKED into the room and over to the television. She jabbed the power button. Immediately after the TV popped on, she turned up the volume. If they were going to have an argument, by God, she didn't want their friends to pick it up.

Ian shut the door, fury in every step. He kept his voice down. He grabbed her close, hugged her to the length of him.

"What the hell do you think you were doing earlier?" Lara whispered the words harshly against his throat, shut down the impulse to take a nip. "All night you've been touching me, stroking me, marking your territory." Making her body sing at a fevered pitch. "You destroyed any opportunity for me to pump Davidenko for information."

"Information? Not like that you don't," he rasped next to her ear, caught her earlobe between wickedly sharp teeth.

"But you arrange to play poker?" Lara closed her eyes, willed herself to stop the heat that raced through her blood. Not this time, damn it. It wasn't going to happen again. The last time they'd gotten into a fight like this they ended up on the floor. "It's too risky a plan."

"It's Texas Holdem. Not a shoot-out at the O.K. Corral." One hand slipped behind her neck, his thumb caressing the underside of her jaw. With the other, Ian loosened the pins in her hair, let it tumble to her shoulders before burying his fingers into the wild tresses.

"With a Russian terrorist, it can turn into the St. Valentine's Day massacre." Lara's head fell back, giving Ian more access.

"What is this about, Red?" Ian played with her bottom lip, nibbling it with his teeth, then soothing it with his tongue. "The fact that it's just me going in there, or the fact that you don't approve of what I'm doing?"

Lara's fingers crept up his chest, slipped under his shirt, popping any buttons in her path. Crisp hair tickled her palm, triggering little electric shocks all the way to her elbow. "I don't think you're using your head—"

Ian's hand slid behind her, tracing the bumps of her spine until she squirmed tight against the hardness between his legs.

"I don't think you're using yours, so hear me out." His voice was a distant hum against her shoulder.

"Fine." Lara gritted her teeth, forcing herself to focus.

"I have two reasons for being at that game tomorrow. One, Novak doesn't want me there."

"How do you know?"

"Body language, my little voice, instinct. Pick one," Ian stated, keeping his voice low and intimate. "But I know he isn't happy about it. Give me a little time and I'll figure out why."

"We don't have time," she murmured, tracing his jawline with her lips. "As it is, we can't make a move until morning."

"You sound like I don't know what's at stake, Lara. I do. You're not going to die and neither will our baby. Or anyone else for that matter."

"What's your second reason?" Giving in to temptation, her hand slipped between them.

"You." He groaned the word, his breath heavy. Slowly, she traced the hard outline under his zipper, knowing the cameras wouldn't see. Her bones dissolved in liquid heat. Lara sagged against him, trembling with need. "Ian, I can't…."

He grabbed her hand, stopped the torture for both of them. "You're going back in."

"Back in where?" Then, Lara understood and she pulled back. Her eyes found his. "Back into Davidenko's suite?" she whispered.

"Novak's," Ian corrected, tipping his forehead against hers and dragging in several deep breaths. "During the poker game. It's the best distraction we have. From the sound of it, Davidenko's friends are heavy hitters—Russian heavy hitters. I'm betting they're Mafia or connected some way to the Mafia."

"Can you say *Godfather?*" Lara kept her tone

low, remembering their earlier conversation. "Novak could be wiping out half the Mafia with the *Katts Smeart.*"

"More than half. Either way, Davidenko's security will be concentrating on keeping those men safe. That means Novak will have his hands full. It will give you time to search for the *Katts Smeart* files."

"You sure know how to turn a girl on, MacAlister—"

Lara stopped short. Her eyes widened as her picture flashed onto the television screen.

"On a lighter note. Rumor has it that Vice President Mercer is going to be a grandfather soon. An unconfirmed report has come in that Lara Mercer, his only daughter, is going to have a baby.

Miss Mercer and Ian MacAlister, son to whiskey king, Quentin MacAlister have been spotted together in Las Vegas."

The anchorman flashed a set of pearly white teeth.

"I'm guessing Miss Mercer, the big question now is, who's the daddy?"

Slowly, Lara broke away and sank onto the couch. The news? How in the hell did she make the news? Lara glanced up, felt the blast from twin blue lasers. "Well, Daddy?"

Without warning, Ian grabbed Lara's hand, yanked her out onto the balcony.

"You're being obvious."

"Too bad," he bit out through clenched teeth.

The wind whipped around them, its icy edges scattering goose bumps down her arms. Lara's body heat plummeted to a deep freeze in one split second.

"How in the hell did the press get a hold of your pregnancy?"

"Downstairs, in the casino's restroom," Lara responded, shivering. It hadn't taken her more than a moment to figure out the source.

"What?"

Quickly Lara explained her encounter with Jenny's mother.

"Who was this again?"

"Some woman, Ian. I didn't ask her name." Lara rubbed her arms, clenched her jaw to keep her teeth from chattering.

Swearing, Ian pulled her against him, used his body to seep warmth into hers.

"It wasn't like I planned to announce it. She had a little girl and a baby. Next thing I know, she was asking me if I had children and I told her I was pregnant."

"Just like that."

"Just like that." Lara frowned, because it was really just like that. In retrospect, the woman had done her a favor. Lara gained a perspective on the pregnancy, decided her priorities. "We ended up talking about morning sickness."

"Morning sickness?"

"And how soon-to-be-fathers can be annoying."

"Not funny, Red."

"Look, either she couldn't keep the secret," she responded, keeping her voice even, "or someone heard us talking. Either way, it was my fault. Not hers. I exposed the baby. I've put it in danger." Lara cleared her throat, trying to unblock the emotion. "God, I so suck at being a mom."

Just that quick Ian's anger dissipated. A mom? Lara called herself a mom. "I think there's a learning curve, all things considered."

With a sigh, he gathered her closer, tucked her head under his chin. "Look, there's nothing we can do about it now, except ride it out."

Lara leaned back until their eyes met. "Thanks," she murmured, then kissed him. A short, spontaneous kiss. One that had nothing to do with the role they were playing. One that left her body tingling. Testing, she did it again. Lingered over his sharp intake of breath.

"Ian," Lara whispered, nipping at his lip. "I—"

She what? She was sorry? It seemed so banal after everything, she realized. He hadn't asked for this. The baby. Novak. She'd gotten him into this.

"Not here, Red. Not like this," Ian responded, his

voice low with anguish or desire—Lara couldn't be sure. He set her away from him, putting a different kind of coldness between them. "Not until this is over."

Chapter Eleven

"Mr. Novak?"

"What?" Anton snapped. The frustration burrowed under his skin, aggravating his temper. After his argument with Xavier, he'd spent all day trying to track down Eos, only to come up empty. Time was running out and so were his options.

He saw Alexei approaching with a teenager by his side. Dressed in low-hanging jeans and a basketball jersey, the kid looked as if he'd just come from a neighborhood school yard, not the casino.

"I caught this guy trying to sneak in here. And since Mr. Davidenko isn't around, I thought I'd bring him to you."

"I understand, Alexei." Novak studied the boy, not pleased when he saw unnatural glitter in the bloodshot eyes. "You're high, aren't you?"

"No—"

"What do you want?"

"I want to cut a deal with Mr. Davidenko."

"A deal?" Anton laughed, the harsh undertone causing the teen to step back. "Mr. Davidenko doesn't make deals with children."

"I have information," he said stubbornly.

"I don't care." Anton turned to Alexei. "Take him downstairs and let him go." He paused for effect. "If he comes back, break his legs."

Alexei started to drag the kid away.

"I saw some couple ripping you off this morning."

Anton turned back, assessing. "Wait, Alexei."

The bodyguard stopped and the boy stumbled. Alexei grabbed him by the shirt to keep him from falling to the floor.

"What's your name, boy?" Anton asked, his features set.

"J.T."

"Alexei, take J.T. to my office," Anton ordered. "I want to have a little chat with him."

"WHO DID YOU SEE?"

"Some guy and his old lady." J.T. shrugged. He wore the arrogance of youth like a badge of honor.

Stupid, but understandable. "What did they look like?"

"Man, it was dark. I couldn't see them in the dark."

"How did you know they were together, then? A couple, I mean?"

"They argued like they were together." J.T. picked up a crystal paperweight from Anton's desk, weighed it in his hand, considered its value. "Like my parents did, before they split. Without the fists flying of course. Or the swearing."

Anton wondered if he'd been that conceited when he'd taken on Mikhail. "Did you hear any names?"

"Sure. Red. He called her Red." J.T. put the paperweight down, cocked his head with superiority. "She called him Ian."

Anton swore. He picked up his phone and dialed the front desk. "Get me Bernard." Then he hit his buzzer.

Alexei opened the door and Anton pointed to the boy. "Give him a hundred dollars—then drop him off downtown." Anton skewered J.T. with his eyes. "If I see you again, I will be the last thing you see. Get me?"

"Yeah."

Anton waved Alexei away.

"This is Bernard." The manager's voice squeaked across the line.

"Bernard, I need to know if Ian MacAlister or Lara Mercer placed anything in our hotel safe."

"Yes, sir. I put it there myself. A black leather briefcase—"

Anton hung up, then dialed another number.

"The briefcase is here. The son of a bitch checked it in to the hotel safe right under our noses. We've a lot to do before the game—" He caught the television screen out of the corner of his eye. "Hold on." He grabbed the remote and turned up the volume.

His frown deepened as the newscaster's words

penetrated his thoughts. "She's pregnant?" Anton laughed, a short harsh blast of air. "Eos is pregnant."

IAN TOOK A DEEP, shuddered breath and let the steam fill his lungs. Sweat ran in long rivulets down his face, stinging his eyes. Perversely, he kept them open—watching the haze thicken, its density crowd him. He was in love with Lara. There was no way around it. And he'd end up losing her, in order to save her.

Somewhere through the fog, a latch clicked. Fresh air rushed in, turning steam into mist, blasting the heat from his skin—leaving a prickly coolness in its wake.

Lara appeared on its heels, her face already flushed from the steam. The slip dress clung to her, a second skin of silk that revealed the sweet lines of her body beneath.

She swung the door wide-open, allowing the heat to dissipate before she moved closer.

"I don't have to prove anything to anyone, Ian. I'm good at what I do."

"No argument there." His voice remained relaxed, but she saw his muscles tighten with caution.

"I've spent my whole life making my own decisions, creating my path in life," she continued as if he hadn't spoken. "In fact, I think we could both agree that I'm used to getting my own way."

She reached over and turned off the steam, deliberately stretching the silk against her already-sweat-damp skin.

"Now that you mention it, Red, a little more flexibility might not hurt."

"Maybe now is the time to start practicing." Stalking him, she took another step closer, then let her gaze skim over the tanned skin and sleek muscles.

An urge to feel him naked against her, caught at her. She shifted forward.

"Lara," Ian warned. He folded his arms across his chest. To stop her perusal maybe? When she tugged the towel from his lap and dropped it to the floor, he couldn't deny his reaction.

"If you're worried about knocking me up, don't," she teased.

"I'm worried about hurting you." He placed a hand on her shoulder, squeezed enough to stop any forward movement. But the tenderness was there, in the depth of his gaze. Her heart fluttered to her throat.

"I don't hurt so easily."

With gentle fingers, he tilted her chin up. "What's this about, Red?"

"It's about you and me," she whispered, glimpsing the tenderness in his gaze, using it as her lifeline. "No more jokes."

With deliberate movements, she eased herself over his legs. "No more lies." Ian caught sight of a pale inner thigh before she slid onto his lap, her legs spread wide to straddle his hips. He felt the tender sweep of her skin against his. The brush of curls against his lower belly.

"No more anger." Lara caught his hand, pressed his palm to her lips for a kiss.

"It's all about this." She laid his palm against her stomach until he felt the slight quiver of muscles beneath.

"And this." She moved his hand against her heart—its beat fast, uneven.

"Lara, I—"

"Shh," she whispered and positioned a finger against his lips. She guided his hand to her leg, placed it just above her ankle. Unhurried, she slid his hand up her calf, closing her eyes briefly when he eased it up and over her knee. "And this," she murmured. Silk gave way, brushed aside by his fingers. He skimmed the soft curve of her thigh, cupped the hollow of her hip.

"Are we clear, MacAlister?" She caught the hem of her dress, pulled it up and over her head. With a careless hand, she dropped the dress, leaving a pool of sapphire at his feet. "Or do I need to be more specific?" Her arms curved around his neck, her eyes found his, their depths burning with an emerald fire.

"Pretty clear." His fingers skimmed the delicate line of her throat, its slope into her shoulder, then followed the inside of her arm. Goose bumps spread.

"Good," she agreed, her breath coming in short, uneven gasps.

Intrigued, his fingers continued to travel, tracing the paths of freckles to the most sensitive parts of her body. He lingered at her inner elbows…her rib cage…the sides of her breasts.

Lara's head tilted back. Ian watched, fascinated by the slow offbeat pulse in the hollow of her throat. He nibbled it, felt the spot flutter beneath his tongue.

Whimpering, she shifted until she cradled his hardness against the soft, wet warmth at the apex of her thighs.

Ian swallowed a groan.

Her fingers snagged his sweat-dampened hair, then tugged him closer to her chest and lifted her breast. "You missed a spot, soldier."

"I don't think so…ma'am." With gentle fingers he cupped each breast, weighing them first, then kneading as if considering. Her throat flexed, her body arched.

Wanting him, but not enough. Not yet. "I've never really been a boob man. You're asking for quite a sacrifice for king and country."

Lara yanked his hair. "I said no jokes."

"Who's joking?" He met her glare, the rasp in his voice betraying his need. His gaze had already drifted, taking in the tiny changes that her pregnancy had brought. Her nipples had darkened, their points extended in two hard beads. The breasts themselves were already filling out, plumper. He imagined each breast heavy with milk.

For his baby.

Male satisfaction poured through him; like gas to

a fire, it ignited an all-consuming possessiveness deep within.

His head dipped low. He nuzzled first one then the other, using his whiskers to rub their sensitive points.

Now that he'd gotten closer, he could see the light blue veins, the way her skin had turned into pale, almost translucent satin. Lightly, he blew air over the peaks, watching, fascinated when each areola puckered in response.

"Ian. *Please.*"

His hands slid under her, deliberately trailing one finger through the swollen folds hidden beneath the triangle of titian curls. She closed her eyes and moaned.

Slowly, he lifted her, holding her suspended. Blood rushed, engorging his own throbbing length.

"Look at me, Lara." Her eyes, heavy lidded with passion, drifted open, only to widen when he settled her over him. The tip of him nudging, his shoulder tightening with the need to plunge himself into her heated depths. "We don't go back. Not from this."

Gasping, Lara clung to his shoulders. "No, not from this." She pushed down, her thigh muscles shaking with need.

Then he was there, sheathed deep.

Ian's head dropped back, his neck corded. He fought the urge to thrust. Not yet, damn it. They weren't finished.

Lara buried her face into his shoulder. Carefully, she rocked back, shuddered when she felt him pulse within her.

"Again," Ian rasped. Their skin was damp with perspiration, the musky scent of sex surrounded them.

She whimpered, but still tilted her hips. This time a little farther, clutching a little tighter. Testing their endurance.

Neither willing to give in.

His body strained for release, driving him toward the edge where relief lay just out of reach. He fought against the pull—holding it back, holding her close. His breath ragged with the effort.

Too soon. He wanted, needed—

"I love you, Ian."

She had whispered the words against his skin, but he'd heard.

Her confession ricocheted through him—shattering his control. With a growl, he let go with one thrust—driving up, flying, exploding.

She cried, tightening around him, seizing him in a fiery spasm of release.

Only long minutes later, with her body still wrapped around his and him still deep within her, did he find her lips with his own.

With a sigh, Lara sank against him. And for the first time since she could remember, reveled in her femininity. "Ian?"

"Hmmm..."

She slipped her hand over his heart, felt the rumble in his chest. "Are you sure you're not a boob man?"

"I'm sure." He chuckled, then kissed the top of her head. "But I've a feeling, over time, you're going to change that."

Although he'd meant to joke, his words had a sobering effect. Tears pricked at her eyes. Over time. Without thinking, she rested her cheek against his chest. "Ian?"

"Hmmm..."

"Don't worry. I won't let our baby die."

NEITHER OF THEM FELT the need to leave the shower. For a long time, Lara stayed curled in Ian's lap, enjoying the stroking and petting. She hadn't been held like that since before she'd been six; it was even longer since she'd felt so cherished and safe.

Soon, though, the shower had chilled to the point Lara couldn't stop shivering. Ian wrapped her in a towel, covering her from shoulder to thigh. Not bothering with his own nakedness, he picked her up and carried her to bed.

Both of them slipped completely under the duvet, cognizant of the fact they were being observed. If they left the hotel room now, it would raise suspicions. They were better off sleeping a few hours.

"You smell good," she murmured, heard him chuckle. Not caring, she took another sinful whiff. "I remember the first time I danced with you. You smelled good then, too. I was eighteen, you were what? Twenty-six? Already a Navy SEAL and full of yourself." She smiled, remembering the stiff, white—very sexy—uniform.

Ian's chin drifted, rubbing her temple and cheek before finally resting against the curve of her neck. "I remember. Ten years isn't that long." Ian slipped the towel from Lara, shoved it out from the covers and threw it to the floor.

His body spooned hers, giving her heat and comfort. While one hand lay protectively across her stomach, the other softly caressed her breast.

"It was your first outing with your dad, wasn't it? A charity event." He rolled his hips, cupping her rear intimately against him.

"Uh-hmm." Lethargy slipped through her, weighing down her limbs, making her eyelids droop.

"I noticed you, too. Too much." Not wanting to wake her, Ian's voice dipped to a husky murmur. "You wore a strapless black dress. With a slit up the side. I wanted to kiss every one of your freckles." In that moment he'd changed. With light fingers, Ian eased away her hair, just enough to place a kiss on the soft hollow of her shoulder.

It had just taken him ten years to figure it out.

Chapter Twelve

Friday, 1130 hours

"Thank you for waiting, Mr. MacAlister." Bernard placed a large safety deposit box in front of Lara and Ian.

"No problem." Ian shifted forward in his chair.

"I'll give you a few minutes to check the contents. Alone."

Lara moved her chair close, and waited for the door to shut. The room had similar features to a police interrogation room. Small, with no windows and one long mirror—two-way most likely. Although most interrogation rooms she'd seen didn't have a round carved, oak wood table with six matching opal-pink velvet chairs.

Ian inserted his key, turned it and opened the lid.

Immediately, the scent of soap pinched at Lara's nose. Soap?

"Ian, the briefcase, it's been—"

Mr. Bernard opened the door; following him in were two men. The first one was tall, all muscle, with thinning hair cropped close to his scalp and a goatee for the badass effect. The other, Lara recognized from Sophia's suite and then later in front of Davidenko's elevator.

"That was definitely a quick moment alone, Bernard."

"Mr. MacAlister, I'm sorry for the interruption. My name is Joseph." The bodyguard's gaze drifted briefly over Ian and Lara had to hide a smile.

The shirt, tie, pants—even Ian's shoes were nothing more than a matte black. The only color he'd allowed was a solid gold tie clip that he'd pulled from the glove compartment of the Hummer. Otherwise, he might have been stamped from the same assembly line as Davidenko's security.

Joseph nodded toward his friend. "This is my associate Alexei. We're here to escort you to the game, sir. Considering the amount of money you're carrying, Mr. Davidenko doesn't want any mishaps along the way."

Lara's hand squeezed Ian's thigh, stopping his response. "And if we're not quite ready?" she asked.

"Then we'd be glad to take your money to the casino room. The gentlemen will be gathering there in a half hour."

Earlier, Lara had chosen her white miniskirt and a matching sleeveless turtleneck sweater. Now she was glad she did. Under the table, she slid up the skirt hem and snagged the switchblade from her thigh.

She hit the mechanism, covered the soft click of the blade with a cough. "Sorry." She shrugged. Keeping her hands hidden, Lara ran the knife across her palm. The pain bit into her, but she absorbed it. Blood, warm and thick, ran through her fingers.

"You'll take my money?" Ian's smile didn't quite reach his eyes. "I don't think so."

Lara tucked the switchblade back against her thigh, then grabbed the chair and scooted back. Immediately she cried out and brought her palm out in the open. Blood oozed from a two-inch cut. "Ian—" Lara showed him the injury "—my hand caught on a nail or something under the chair."

"Mademoiselle, I'm so sorry." Bernard hurried over and gave her his handkerchief. "It's clean I promise you."

"Thank you." Lara gripped the cloth and turned to Ian. "Darling, let Mr. Joseph take your money. I believe we can trust Mr. Davidenko's associates."

Joseph's dark eyes narrowed with surprise. "I can assure you, Mr. MacAlister, your money is quite safe with us."

"All right," Ian handed over the briefcase. "But I'll keep the key to the lock. After all it is a million dollars, right?"

"I need you to sign these release forms, Joseph." Bernard handed him some papers, then pulled a pen from his inside suit pocket. "We're required to have documentation that you've taken possession again of Mr. MacAlister's money."

With a quick hand, Joseph signed.

"Tell your boss I'll be joining him soon. After I take care of Lara's injury."

Moments later, Ian and Lara were out the door and in the lobby. "Okay, Red. Are you going to tell me why you sliced your hand up?"

"The money, it's contaminated," she said urgently. "We need to go to the gift shop first."

Like most gift shops, the Bontecou's carried toiletries. Lara located them quickly, in the back corner.

"Start from the top," Ian demanded.

"The briefcase smelled of soap." Lara ran her gaze over the different labels until she located an antibiotic cream that held no scent.

"What the hell is that supposed to mean?"

"Someone washed it. And there's only one reason why."

"Are you saying the money has been treated with the *Katts Smeart?*"

"Why else would the briefcase smell like soap?" She snagged the biggest tube of cream, then looked for the bandages. Her palm throbbed, but she ignored it. "Someone washed the leather sometime between last night in the desert and today."

"I rigged the briefcase lock, Lara. Remember? Before we checked in to the hotel. I would've known if anyone had tampered with it."

"Not if they contaminated the money before we got a hold of it in the desert," Lara said. "The safety deposit box is theirs. They'd have access to the case."

Lara spotted the cashier. "Hold on."

Within moments, she returned with her purchases in a paper bag.

"We need to go to the bar, Ian." She grabbed his hand, hurried across the lobby. The bar, dark and deserted because of the early-morning hour, was perfect for privacy.

They found a corner booth. Lara scooted in, surprised when Ian sat next to her.

"Let me see your hand."

"It's the least of our worries." Lara showed him the cut. "We just lost our opportunity to grab the money and disappear."

"I wouldn't have taken it anyway." Ian grabbed the paper bag and took out the antibacterial cream. "There's no guarantee that the priest or Novak used all the *Katts Smeart* on the money. Novak could have more. For that matter, he could be working with Davidenko."

"I don't need the cream, Ian." Lara pulled on her hand, but Ian tightened his grip.

"The cameras don't know that, Red. And you can bet we're being watched." Ian opened the tube, then squeezed the cream onto the cut. "Joseph followed Novak yesterday to the church."

"Joseph? For protection or surveillance?" A calloused finger brushed the inside of her wrist, sending a jolt of electricity up her arm.

Ian glanced up when he felt the tremble, his eyes darkened with awareness. "When this is over, Red..."

Lara nodded, not willing to risk her voice wavering.

Ian let go and grabbed the box of bandages. He pulled one out. "Joseph could've killed Father Xavier after Novak and the priest parted company. Novak might not even know Father Xavier is dead."

"Whatever the answer, we can't make a move until we've retrieved *Katts Smeart* and the antidote."

With gentle fingers, Ian placed the bandage over Lara's cut. "The question is, how did Novak contaminate Armand's money and why? Unless Armand was in on it, too. Novak could've been selling the *Katts Smeart* to Armand."

"That doesn't make sense. The odds were pretty high that you'd use gas to knock out Novak. Remember, he was ready for you with the oxygen tube. If Armand was part of their deal, he'd have been prepared for you, too," Ian reasoned. "No, we're missing a key element here."

"Key element," Lara repeated, then gasped. "Ian, Father Xavier said the rosary was the key."

Ian frowned. "The beads. He could've made them out of the antidote."

"No," Lara answered. "I took them to a jeweler in downtown Vegas before I headed to the desert. The beads are definitely freshwater pearls."

"The rosary is what contaminated you. The key to your situation—"

"But what if it's not? What if he meant something else?" she wondered aloud, struggling to fit the puzzle pieces together.

"Are you saying it might be a real key?"

"If it is, we've been looking in the wrong place." Lara squeezed his hand. "Father Xavier would never have put the church in danger. I'm sure of it."

"Maybe, maybe not. But we're running out of time. You either search Novak's office or—"

"The church." Lara decided grimly. "If I run out of time, I'd rather it be at a church."

Ian stared at her, knowing it was her choice. "Start with the priest's quarters, then the church. I'll deal with the poker game. And Novak."

"Ian, you need to put this antibacterial cream on your hands." Lara grabbed the tube, winced at the sting of her palm. "It might not protect you from the contaminated money, but it's worth a shot."

Ian shoved the tube into his pocket.

"If they see it, just tell them you forgot to leave it in the suite when you fixed my hand."

"Don't worry about me, Red. I'll be fine."

"I can't help worrying," Lara replied, refusing to give in to the tears that gathered behind her eyes.

"The other players will be exposed. We'll need to keep them contained."

"I'll handle that." Ian reached into his pocket, then tossed her his car keys. "Take the Hummer to the church and be careful."

Lara leaned over and allowed herself a long, lingering kiss against his lips. "Remember, when this is over…"

"GOOD AFTERNOON, Mr. MacAlister, Miss Mercer." Joseph greeted them the moment Ian and Lara stepped off the elevator.

"Hello," Lara responded, letting a slight smile tease her lips.

"I'm sorry, Miss Mercer, but the poker game is closed to everyone except those playing. Strict rules."

"No worries," Lara reassured him. "I'm just here to send my guy off in style, then go spend some of his money."

Joseph nodded and then raised the metal detector wand in his hand. "Do you mind?" he asked Ian.

"Not at all," Ian managed, then deliberately stepped toward Joseph and away from Lara.

Joseph quickly ran the metal wand over Ian, then nodded.

"Well, goodbye, darling." When Ian returned to Lara's side, she snuggled into his arms and kissed him.

Ian felt her slip the knife in his front pocket. "Good luck," she said.

Ian kissed her nose. "You, too." But expression left no doubt to his warning. *Be careful.*

Lara pulled away. "You boys have fun now." She waved, then stepped into the elevator.

"Quite a woman."

Ian watched the doors close before he acknowledged Davidenko's remark. "Yes, she is."

"I'm glad you could join us." Mikhail Davidenko crossed the entry and offered his hand. Ian returned the handshake, reasonably sure that no one had touched the money yet. "What can I get you to drink?"

Ian's lips twitched. "Whiskey."

"Yes, yes, of course," Davidenko said, then snapped his fingers. "Anton, please get Mr. MacAlister—"

"Ian."

Mikhail studied him for a moment, then nodded. "Ian…a glass of whiskey. Straight?"

"Yes. Make it a double."

"You drink whiskey like I drink vodka," Davidenko laughed.

Ian accepted the glass from Novak. "Good to see you again, Novak."

"You, too," Novak said smoothly. "Bernard called and told me about Miss Mercer's mishap. I hope she's okay?"

"She's fine. Nothing that a few bandages couldn't solve. You should have that chair checked, though."

"We did." Novak's eyes glinted. "But Bernard found nothing."

"Really?" Ian lifted an eyebrow. "You sure he had the right chair?"

LARA HEADED FOR the main door of the casino. She glanced at her watch. Just past noon. Lara figured that gave her less than three hours to find the antidote.

Time was ticking. But what she'd done last night, she wouldn't take back. If they had only that night then so be it. Her heart squeezed just a little. Ian was going to be part of their child's life whether she wanted him there or not. The trouble is she wanted him there. Too much.

"Miss Mercer." Lara swung around and saw a man, midthirties, with a small neat mustache and wearing the standard black suit. "Yes?"

"I'm Maurice, the hotel concierge." He pointed to the front entrance. "There are several reporters outside waiting for you."

Lara glanced through the French doors. "Maurice, would it be possible to have Mr. MacAlister's Hummer brought around to the employees' entrance?"

"Yes, mademoiselle."

Since becoming the Vice President's daughter, she'd had her fair share of interviews. However, Lara had always done a good job of keeping her answers geared to the political, not the personal.

Lara slipped the concierge some money. "Discreetly? They're probably watching his car."

"I've had experience, Miss Mercer." Maurice

smiled. "If you'll follow me, we can leave through the kitchen."

"Of, course—" A flash of black caught her eyes. She looked, but the features blurred through the etched windows. "I'll meet you there, Maurice."

Quickly, Lara stepped outside.

Flashbulbs sparked, microphones appeared in bouquets. Most of them shoved mere inches from her face.

"Miss Mercer, is it true you're pregnant?"

"Is the baby's father Ian MacAlister?"

"How far along are you?"

"Miss Mercer, what did your father say when you told him you were pregnant with his first grandchild?"

"Miss Mercer, where's Mr. MacAlister?"

"Are you planning on getting married?"

"Look, guys." Lara held her hand up, stopping the influx of questions. "You're not going to get a story today. So be patient and keep watching from the sidelines for a while. Then when the time is right, I'll answer your questions." Her eyes scanned the crowd, checking features.

"Miss Mercer?"

Lara stopped, her eyes homed in on a woman reporter.

She wore a slim-fitting suit. A crisp, light vanilla number that showed a tad more thigh and cleavage than most on camera, but in no way sacrificed her professional appeal. Now free from the band, her hair hung straight, like a black sheet of silk that stopped just inches past a tight, determined jaw.

The baby, Lara noted, had been replaced by a microphone. Still, Lara had no trouble recognizing the woman from the restroom. "You are?"

"Sarah Kwong, *Las Vegas Courier.*" The slant of her almond green eyes deepened with caution, but still she stepped forward.

Lara arched an eyebrow. "A little low using children, don't you think, Ms. Kwong?"

"Niece and nephew," Sarah replied. "Call it fate. My sister was in another stall." Her chin lifted, tempting Lara to knock it back down. "You're not the type to hold grudges, I hope."

"Grudges? Sometimes." Lara's lips thinned. "I just haven't decided if this is one of those times. Give me a month. Then give me a call," she said, pleased when the other woman's jaw went slack with shock.

Lara turned on her heel and walked away.

QUENTIN MACALISTER cherished three things in life. His family. The slow bite of a fine single malt whiskey. And poker.

By the time Ian had turned double digits in age, he'd become his dad.

"So, MacAlister..." asked a portly man, with a blotchy face and heavy jowls. "You like poker, eh?" Bogdon Kuznetsova tossed fifty thousand dollars into the middle of the table.

"Yes." Ian glanced at his cards. A pair of tens. "But there are many things I like more." He paused and added his fifty to the growing pile of money in the middle of the table. "And less."

Everyone gave a perfunctory laugh, which did nothing to ease the tension-filled air.

For the first hour, things remained typically quiet. But soon liquor and curiosity loosened the conversation.

Over the last thirty or more years, Russian organized crime syndicates in America had jumped into overdrive. Growing at a steadier incline than most other organized syndicates, including the Italian and the Chinese.

The fact that Ian seemed to be the only non-Russian, non-Mafia of the six sitting at the table, told him how much power Davidenko held with these men.

"There are many things I like more, too," said Orel Petrov, the player to Ian's immediate left. A bull of a man with thick eyelids and a scar that slashed from the left corner of his mouth up to his temple. He was a known arms merchant and money launderer. Because of the scar, when he smiled, his lips curved into a lopsided sneer. "But that will come later, won't it, Mikhail?" He raised the bet another fifty thousand, then leaned toward Ian. "Mikhail is known for his stable of working girls. Beautiful, accommodating and best of all, they don't speak Russian."

"Nothing is worse than a woman who can speak Russian," Sergei Uspensky responded, a meaty guy with a unibrow and a missing earlobe. He threw down his cards, disgusted. "I fold."

The last Ian heard, Uspensky was the Russian go-to guy for drug trafficking, white slavery and prostitution.

"Why are Russian-speaking women so bad?" Ian asked, only because it was expected.

"Russian is perfect for song, for poetry, even for opera. But not for anger," Uspensky responded. "Too many comrades go deaf from screeching Russian wives."

The men laughed, huge booming shouts that reminded Ian of drunken sailors. Ian joined in, because that, too, was expected.

"Anton, another drink. *Pozhaluista.*" Please.

"Certainly, Mr. Toltov," Novak answered. But Ian saw the slight hesitation before he took the offered glass.

Ian glanced across the table. Vas Toltov, rumored the Godfather of the Russian Mafia, was a soft-spoken man. Older, almost eighty, with a frail build and sharp, bony features.

Tolstov had massacred two families, simply because the eldest daughter of one had declined to date Toltov's grandson. At the time, she'd been engaged to be married.

Both families of the engaged couple died the

night before the wedding. Fifteen people butchered in their homes.

Novak, for the last two hours had watched the game from the bar. He smoked the occasional cigarette and ran interference when one of the men needed food or drink. Ian hadn't seen any waitresses. Or other bodyguards, not even for the Russian guests. Only Alexei and Novak were present.

A rule of Davidenko's? Or a custom of the game?

"I don't think Ian has need for more beautiful women," Davidenko commented. He folded his cards, then reached for the handful of chips he'd brought to the table. With one hand, he shuffled his chips with a practiced cadence. Boring, consistent. "He has a woman already."

"Who's to say he can't have more?" Petrov questioned.

Good poker required a steady rhythm of bets, raises and folds. A good poker player never changed that rhythm.

Davidenko was a good poker player.

"I think his woman would," Davidenko continued. "Especially since she might be pregnant."

Ian understood the statement. Fear crept down his back. Davidenko was letting Ian know he was aware of Ian's Achilles' heel. Ian smiled easily. "That's the rumor."

"I call," Toltov said, and tossed in his money. "Then the pregnancy is only a rumor, Ian?" Toltov asked, his blue eyes keen with interest. "If it were fact, we would toast you and your new family."

Ian met the bet and called. For the past two hours, no great sums of money had been won by anyone. Small amounts had changed hands—enough that everyone at the table had touched the contaminated money.

"I'm not in the market for a new family," Ian replied with derision, letting them know that Lara didn't mean anything to him.

Uspensky, the designated dealer for this hand, flopped the first three cards. A seven, six and three. All different suits.

"All in," Petrov said with a leer. "That's—" he counted his money "—four hundred and forty-five thousand to you," he said to Toltov.

Toltov vacillated, then threw in his cards. "I think you're bluffing, but I don't have anything strong enough to prove you don't have a straight, comrade."

"Too much for me," Kuznetsova wheezed. He folded his cards, leaned back and lit a cigar.

Ian deliberately waited for a moment to make his bet. It was time to test the waters. "I call," he said easily.

Ian glanced at Petrov, saw the man blink. *Gotcha.* Without breaking his expression, Ian flipped over his cards. "A pair of tens."

Petrov stood. "You call me with a pair of tens!" He let out a stream of curse words. "I raise you four hundred thousand and you call me with a pair of tens. You think I don't have the straight?"

Ian leaned back, deliberately not saying a word.

"He must think that or he wouldn't have called you," Toltov stated. "Lay your cards down, Orel."

Petrov threw down his cards. A jack and four—off suit. "All I need is a five for my straight. Or a jack to beat your pair," he sneered.

Ian said nothing.

Uspensky turned the fourth card. "Two of spades. That gives you a pair, Orel."

Ian waited, calm. He'd watched these men for the past few hours, learned the Russian's tells. Orel had been bluffing, and although the odds favored Ian, they both understood either could win.

Uspensky flipped the last card. "Another eight. You both have two pair, but the ten-eights beat the eight-twos. The Scot wins, Orel."

Davidenko got up and patted Ian on the back. "Good hand, son." Then he turned to Petrov. "If you want to play the next hand, Orel, stop swearing and put up more money. The boy beat you fair and square. We all knew you were bluffing."

Petrov scowled and Ian kept quiet. He didn't touch the money.

"Here, Mr. Petrov," Novak offered smoothly and handed Orel a double shot of vodka. Orel looked at Ian, then grabbed the glass from Novak. He swallowed the liquor in one gulp, his eyes never leaving Ian's.

After a few moments, he slammed the glass onto the table. “Good call, MacAlister.” The big man raised his hand.

“Thank you.” Ian nodded, shook the man’s hand, recognizing—in a span of a few seconds—he’d come close to dying.

After, he pulled in his winnings.

Chapter Thirteen

Friday, 1200 hours, Noon

St. Stan's housed their priests behind the rectory in a small three-story adobe brick building that backed up to a narrow alley way.

Lara didn't have time for caution. So instead she parked the Hummer behind the building, against the residence's back walk and directly below a second-story window.

A dog barked from down the alley. On its heels came a cat's screech and the rattle of metal garbage cans. After a quick glance, she climbed on the vehicle's roof. She wrapped her jacket around the tire iron she'd grabbed earlier from the back of the Hummer. With one sharp jab, she broke the glass, cringed at the sharp echo, then scraped the jagged edges down to the window frame. Quickly, she threw the jacket on the sill, pushed back a mud-brown gingham curtain and hoisted herself in.

Old lamps, television and couch decorated what looked to be a bedroom turned den. One wall contained a built-in bookcase. A montage of books and picture frames filled its shelves.

Deliberately, she left her gun holstered, not wanting to take the chance on shooting an innocent. Lara opened the door, listening for movement before she stepped lightly into the hall.

Five doors lined the hall, including the television room. Three bedrooms and one bathroom, Lara reasoned.

She sidled up to the first and looked in. Top level stereo equipment took up one wall while compact discs of Bon Jovi and Def Leppard lay scattered on the bed. Not quite Father Xavier's taste, she assumed, but definitely a priest she wanted to meet.

The second bedroom, although orderly, contained very little. A maple dresser, matching desk and a twin bed covered with a textured white bedspread. With quick, long strides she walked to the dresser and opened the first drawer. On top of a neat stack of boxer shorts sat several prescription bottles.

Lara read the labels. Erlotinib? Analgesics? A few more Lara didn't recognize. All with Father Xavier's name on the prescription.

Cancer. Father Xavier had been dying of lung cancer.

"No wonder you said it was too late," she murmured. With a quiet efficiency, Lara finished searching that drawer, shoving back the stray socks and handkerchiefs, before moving on to the others.

After the last one proved unsuccessful, Lara stood and surveyed the room. "Okay, Father, what did you do with the *Katts Smeart?*"

Lara didn't expect to actually find the formula in the bedroom, but she'd hoped to find a clue as to where he'd hidden it. A safe deposit key, a note, a business card.

A business card. Lara opened the closet door. Several suits lined a four-foot pole. From dark priest garb to everyday casual suits and pants.

Lara started with the casual items, systematically searching the pockets and seams.

Nothing.

The scent of mothballs and cedar tickled her nose. Irritated, Lara rubbed it, then brushed the hair back from her forehead. What was it with older people and moth—

Lara froze. Cedar. Where did the cedar come from? She ran her hand over the shelf above. Empty.

She glanced down and didn't see any shoes but a small braided rug lay bunched in the closet's back corner.

Lara grabbed the rug and pulled. Underneath, a cedar box, the size of a shoe box, skidded across the hardwood floor.

Lara sat cross-legged on the floor and pulled the box into her lap. For a moment, she listened.

Confident that no one had discovered her entry, Lara lifted the lid. Old pictures, some color, most black and white, filled the inside. Mostly of family, some of places. Russia, China, New York. Under the pictures, she found transfer papers from different churches. A birth certificate, a passport. Lara riffled through to the bottom. Father Xavier would have a separate stash for his government passports and travel documents, false or otherwise.

When Lara shut the lid, a photo caught under the latch. The picture was a woman, a pretty brunette dressed in a smart suit, slim fitting and short. Straight from the nineteen seventies. In front of her stood a little boy—not more than three. Cute button nose, thick shaggy hair. Brown flowered shirt and corduroy jumpsuit. She'd imagined Christel dressing Ian in similar—

Goose bumps tripped up Lara's spine, left the tiny hairs of her neck on end. Slowly, she turned the picture over.

Katia and Anton. Presidio, California. 1973.

In her mind she pictured Father Xavier and Anton together—their broad foreheads, the identical blunt chins.

Father and son.

But the eyes, they were different. The little

boy's eyes were blue, like his mother's. Bright, clear—innocent.

If he had a family, why become a priest? Unless Father Xavier, like her father, had sacrificed his family for duty—

Lara glanced again at the picture, finally understanding.

Father Xavier hadn't sacrificed his family, he'd sacrificed his son.

DAVIDENKO DEALT two cards to each player. In the last hour, small pots had been won and lost. Ian had folded most hands, using the time to study the group of men.

After the huge pot Ian had won against Petrov—and survived—he seemed to have been accepted.

The men talked of sports, women and, to Ian's surprise, wrestling. But never did any mention business.

And not once did Novak enter the conversation.

Ian tipped the edge of his cards. Eight of diamonds and six of clubs. It was time to make another move. "I call the fifteen and raise thirty thousand more."

Petrov swore and threw his cards down. "I fold."

Uspensky studied Ian, his unibrow raised. "What do you have, Boy?"

Ever since Ian won against Petrov, Boy seemed to become his nickname.

Ian shrugged.

"You have something." Uspensky smiled revealing two gold canine teeth. "I think I will fold and watch."

Davidenko glanced at his cards in one hand, while he continued to shuffle his small stack of chips with the other.

Shuffle, shuffle, pause. The rhythm had set the tone for the game.

"I'm in." Davidenko placed his forty-five thousand into the pot.

"I fold," Toltov announced, then he, too, sat back to observe.

Kuznetsova sighed. "I'll call. But I'm not happy about it."

Davidenko waited until Kuznetsova placed his money in the middle before he turned the first three cards. "Jack of hearts, four of hearts and seven of clubs."

Kuznetsova studied the cards for a moment. "I'll bet forty thousand," he decided and counted out the bills.

Petrov snorted. "You're chasing a flush, aren't you, Bogdon?"

Bogdon Kuznetsova grinned. "It will cost them forty grand to find out, comrade."

"I call and raise another forty thousand," Ian commented, already pushing his money into the table's center.

Uspensky laughed. "I think the boy is on to you, too, Bogdon."

"I call and raise another two hundred thousand," Davidenko replied. "If you want to chase your flush, Bogdon, you have to buy your next card."

Kuznetsova swore, then tossed his hand in. "It is not worth it. I'll let you and the boy fight it out, Mikhail. While I drink your vodka."

There was a burst of laughter around the table. Ian waited until it died down. "I'll pay the money to see the next one." He slid in his two hundred thousand.

Petrov let out a slow whistle. "That puts the pot over five hundred thousand, Mikhail."

The derision in Petrov's comment told Ian the Russian would like nothing better than to see Ian lose.

"So let's see what we have, yes?" Davidenko tapped the cards.

The room grew silent. With a half million at stake, all wanted to see how it played out.

Ian placed the older man with a Jack in his hand. With another Jack on the table, that would give Davidenko top pair over Ian's eight and six.

Davidenko turned the next card. "Ace of diamonds."

Shuffle, shuffle, pause.

Satisfaction rose through Ian. Davidenko lagged on the pause a split second longer than usual. It was a subtle tell, one Ian had picked up on earlier in the afternoon.

Davidenko didn't have the ace.

"All in," Ian said, his tone void of emotion. "Seven hundred and eighty thousand."

Davidenko studied Ian's face. "You have it, don't you?"

Ian remained quiet, knowing he'd played Davidenko well. It was best to let the older man think about the previous hands and make his decision.

Davidenko swore. "I fold." Without pretense he flipped his cards over, revealing a Jack and a nine of spades. "I'm not going to give you any more money on a pair of aces."

Ian reached for the money.

Petrov placed his hand on Ian's arm, stopping Ian midmotion. "Aren't you going to show us, Boy?" Petrov said. "It's the least you can do."

Ian's muscles tightened. "Sure, why not." With his free hand, he reached for his cards.

Deliberately, he flipped them in the middle of the table.

"Eight, six of different suits," Petrov remarked, amazed. "The boy bluffed you, Mikhail."

The others said nothing, but all watched.

"Not bad, Ian. But I think you forgot this." Davidenko tossed a pin-size transmitter onto the pile of money—the same one Ian planted in Davidenko's window.

"I think I could have liked you, Boy," Petrov commented, his meaty hand tightening like a vice on Ian's arm.

The hair on the back of Ian's neck prickled, but the

warning came too late. Shock waves slammed him between the shoulder blades, paralyzed his muscles.

Ian tried to stand, caught another jab of the Taser under his ribs. Like lightning—it arced, splintered, then seared.

Without a sound, Ian slipped into unconsciousness.

Chapter Fourteen

Lara stepped from Father Xavier's bedroom, determined to get back to the hotel—

A soft ping hit the air moments before the door pane splintered inches from her ear. A silencer pistol. She dropped to her knees. Another ping hit the air and a chunk of the door disappeared.

Lara snagged her gun, squeezed off a few rounds into the shadows.

"I know you don't have much ammunition with you, Miss Mercer."

"Hello, Joseph," she answered, not surprised. She aimed her gun at the voice, fired. Heard a curse.

"You're at the wrong end of the hall. Which means you didn't have to come through the window. Who gave you the security code, Joseph? Novak?"

"Does it matter? If you give me the *Katts Smeart* files, I'll go." His voice drifted from a different spot, closer to her position. Close enough for her to catch the thick, sweet scent of his aftershave.

"Yeah, sure you will." Lara fired, heard a pair of knees hit the hardwood floor. She snickered. "Novak must have promised you a big piece of Davidenko's business. I could've sworn you two didn't like each other." Lara scooted army style toward Father Xavier's window. Two stories above concrete didn't make a safe jump, even if she was ready to run.

Which she wasn't. She dropped her clip, checked the rounds. Only a few bullets left. With a sharp tug she brought up the window and punched out the screen.

The adobe left no grooves for climbing but, just above the window she discovered a narrow fire escape ladder that led to the roof.

"Davidenko is old. Set in his ways." The voice was almost on her now.

With a short prayer, she emptied her clip of bullets into the doorway, then grabbed the sill and hoisted herself out.

She jumped, caught the bottom iron rung. The metal, frying-pan hot from the sun, burned her fingers. Lara ignored the blistered heat against her skin, the painful burn in her shoulders.

As if in an obstacle course, she scrambled up the ladder. Bullets strafed the wall, tiny shards of cement stinging her face. When she reached the top, she threw herself over the edge and onto the graveled tar. Grit scraped her cheek, cut her lip. Annoyed, she wiped the blood away.

Positioned in the far corner was the stairway entrance. In its shadow, a large heating and cooling unit.

Not much cover. "Damn." She hadn't come this far to lose now. In a millisecond, Lara took in the situation, planned her strategy.

Her gaze dropped to an old mop and bucket propped by the air-conditioning unit. Within moments, she'd grabbed both and dived behind the unit, happy when the whir of the motor covered the sound of her footsteps.

Lara counted to ten, then threw the bucket behind her. A few moments later, the scent of musk aftershave drifted toward her.

Lara stepped out, caught the giant unaware. She brought the mop handle down hard on his arm. Joseph grunted in pain, his revolver hit the ground and skidded to her feet. She grabbed it and fired.

Click. Click.

Disgusted, Lara threw the gun down. "I guess we do this the hard way." She hit the mop's end with her foot, shooting the pole up and into her hands.

"Unless, of course, you hand over the *Katts Smeart,*" Joseph acknowledged, his body semi-crouched for attack.

His reach was twice hers and his weight more than double. One look at the meaty hands told her if they got to her neck, she was dead. "You're out of luck. I didn't find anything in Father Xavier's room."

"Then, as you said, we do this the hard way, eh?"

"Bring it on, big guy." She flexed her wrist, brought the tip of the pole back like a baseball bat.

A high-pitched ring hit the air. Joseph's cell phone.

"You're not going to answer that, are you?" she quipped, then rolled to the balls of her feet. Black belt techniques were out. Dirty street fighting—definitely in.

"Come on, sugar." She waved her fingers, motioning him forward. All coolness and calculation. "I'm ready to kick some Neanderthal ass."

Without warning, Joseph charged.

Lara met him halfway, then hit the deck, sliding. Gravel scraped, then burned her thigh. She slammed into the enforcer's legs, knocking them out from under him, like two bowling pins in an alley.

The big man stumbled, but didn't fall. She rammed the stick into his concrete stomach, heard the hollow thump and his grunt of pain.

Lara didn't stop. She scrambled to her feet. Using the stick for balance she pole-vaulted toward him, twisted in a reverse spinning roundhouse. Her heel hit his throat. Felt the windpipe give, the man choke.

But he was fast. Faster than she'd imagined.

With one meaty fist he grabbed her leg, twisted it back. Lara cried out. The bones ground against cartilage, white-hot pain skewered her from knee to hip.

Lara shifted, brought the mop handle up. Without the support she crashed to the deck, shoulder first. Gravel flayed her shoulder, shredding the skin.

Lara rammed the mop handle into his crotch. Heard the air hiss from his lungs, the howl when he hit the asphalt.

Slowly, she uncoiled and stood. The wind hit her shoulder, setting the scrape ablaze.

She'd dealt with worse—and uglier. She eyed Joseph. "You should always wear protection, idiot. Don't know what you might catch."

Gripping the stick like a club, she brought it down on his head. At the last second, he blocked the hit with his forearm, grabbed the handle and wrenched it from her grasp.

Breathing heavily, he came up on his knees. "You, bitch!" With one twist, he snapped the pole into two jagged spears. "Are we done with the toys?" He threw the wooden pieces on the ground between them.

"Not yet." Lara gauged the distance to the broken mop handle.

"Did I tell you, Miss Mercer?" Joseph snarled. "I specialize in killing pregnant women."

"Not anymore, you don't," Lara hissed. Temper drove her now. And retribution. For Sophia. For her baby. Lara dived for the nearest stick, snatched it, then rolled.

An instant later, she came up beneath him, her back blocking his chest. His arm came around her neck, then squeezed against her windpipe. But this time she was ready.

He wasn't Davidenko, but he'd pay all the same.

Lara shifted forward, taking the giant off balance. In one steady motion, she brought the stick full circle, tucked it under her arm and shoved back. The jagged point speared the enforcer's chest. The wood jerked, punctured skin and muscle, caught against bone.

Joseph wheezed. His arm dropped and he struggled to sit back.

"Remember Sophia?" Lara's voice dripped venom. With one hand she held him in place. With the other, she jammed the pole deeper, pushed up and through.

Blood gurgled in the back of his throat, his muscles went lax against her shoulder blades.

She let go of the stick and scrambled out from under him. Weakly, his big hands tugged the wood, trying to break free. With one last surge of strength, he pulled it out and held the spear, now crimson with blood. For a moment he tried to speak, but only a soft choking sound reached her.

Then the big man fell forward, dead.

Pain ground into Lara's hip, and her shoulder throbbed. But damn it, she was alive. And that creep wasn't.

A series of rings hit the air.

"I'll get that." Lara patted Joseph's pants, found the cell and took it out.

"Mercer."

There was a long pause. "Miss Mercer, now this is a surprise."

In the distance Lara heard sirens. "For Joseph, too, I suspect. He's dead, Novak." She limped toward the fire escape, glanced up the street. Several police cars raced toward the church, their red and blue strobes flashing.

"I certainly underestimated you, didn't I?"

"Looks like it." She swung down the side of the building to the fire escape ladder and started down. "Where's your boss?"

"With the father of your baby."

Lara stopped midstep. Smug bastard.

"You don't really believe those rumors, do you, Novak?" Lara continued down, then forgetting her injury, jumped the final few feet. She winced when the pain lanced through her hips.

"I think you should know MacAlister is currently unconscious and tied to a chair."

Lara made her way to the Hummer. If Novak tied Ian to a chair, he wouldn't stay tied for long. Which meant, he might get himself killed before she could get back.

"The plan is to remove chunks of skin and feed them to Davidenko's pet piranha." Novak paused. "You see, I've grown impatient, Miss Mercer. I want that antidote."

Lara glanced at her purse on the seat. "I have the antidote." Without stopping, she jammed the key into the ignition and turned. The engine roared. She threw the gear into drive and punched the gas. The squeal of tires blended with the growing sound of sirens. "I'm going to ram it down your throat."

"I'm counting on it," Novak responded.

"Why? Have you been exposed, too?"

There was a long enough pause on the other side for Lara to know she'd guessed right. "Lucky for you, I answered the phone." Mentally, she crossed her fingers praying she read Father Xavier right.

"If you want to find your man in one piece, I suggest—"

Lara watched the police cars race past. "You touch one hair on his head, Novak, and you'll never see the antidote. I mean it. We can all die together. And you can kiss your new Russian empire goodbye—especially now that your partner is dead."

"Joseph told you."

"He didn't have to. I had to go through the window. He had the security code." Lara took a corner sharp, punched the gas and almost slid into a moving van. "Which one of you killed your father, Novak? Which one of you killed Father Xavier?"

"You found much more than the antidote, didn't you?" After a long pause, he said, "You have a half hour to get back here. And then we'll start negotiating MacAlister's life for the formula and antidote. You bring anyone with you, he's dead."

Chapter Fifteen

Pain exploded through Ian's jaw, ricocheting through his skull, forcing his eyes open.

"You're awake." Novak sat at the poker table, his pistol pointed at Ian. No Russian friends, no money on the table.

"Seems so," Ian said, tasting blood. After a quick check with his tongue, he found the split inside his cheek.

Ian tested his arms, found them tied behind his back. Cold steel cut into his wrists. With a grim satisfaction, he shifted. Plastic crunched beneath his feet. Ian glanced down, saw the tarp, and then Davidenko. The Russian's eyes lay open; his throat was slit and oozing blood.

"Looking for this?" Novak held up the switchblade. "It certainly does come in handy, doesn't it?" Novak threw the knife at Davidenko, amused when it imbedded in the dead man's chest.

"We found this, too." Novak held up the tube of

antibacterial cream. "I assume you used it to block the *Katts Smeart.*"

"That and a few trips to the bathroom," Ian reasoned, then nodded at Davidenko. "Is this a new form of going postal?"

"Not quite," Novak responded, his features slanting into cruel lines. "More like a corporate takeover. Mikhail ceased to serve his purpose."

"And his Russian pals?"

"Gone. They split your winnings and left long before Davidenko died. But you won't have to worry about them. Not for long anyway." Novak nodded to Armand's briefcase in the center of the table. "I kept a portion of the contaminated money."

"What did you do, tell Davidenko I had the formula?"

"Davidenko had become suspicious of me." Novak shrugged. "So Joseph told him you'd been asking questions, trying to find out where Sophia had gone."

Alexei crossed over to the bar and sat, but his gaze never left Ian.

Ian had grown up the middle child of an overachieving family. A person couldn't survive that without developing some antagonizing skill. "I killed Yuri, Alexei. I snapped his neck."

Alexei remained silent, but hatred glittered in his coal-black eyes.

Ian glanced at Novak. "You trained them well. Do they roll over, too?"

"No, but they do bite, so I'd be careful." Novak's lips twisted with derision.

"Where's your other man? Viktor?"

"Waiting in my helicopter."

"He might have quite a wait ahead of him." Ian looked at the clock, saw Lara had less than two hours in her incubation period. "You've been organizing this takeover for quite some time."

"Actually, this whole plan was my father's idea."

"Your father?" Ian kept his expression blank, but his muscles tensed.

"The good Father Xavier." Novak smiled. "Your girlfriend figured it out. She's on her way now to save you." He paused, his eyes hooded. "Times certainly have changed, haven't they? The woman coming to the rescue."

"Beats dying."

"The ultimate sacrifice—to die for a loved one," Novak commented. "My father believed that."

"So it was suicide?"

"Oh no," Novak acknowledged, regret hollowing his words. "I killed him. He forced me, by deciding that, after all this, I wasn't worth the sacrifice. He drew a gun on me in the hotel room. Only he miscalculated his fragility."

"So you what? Grabbed the gun, shoved it under your father's chin and pulled the trigger?"

"Pretty much." Novak stood, then made his way around the bar. "Davidenko's best vodka." Novak took a bottle from beneath the counter. "I'd offer you some, except—" Novak shrugged "—why waste good vodka."

"Where is Joseph? In the fish tank?" Ian pushed the handcuffs up over his wrist, ignoring the scrape against the bone.

"No," Novak remarked, then poured the vodka. "But he is dead. Seems your girlfriend killed him."

Ian smiled, shifted back into his chair. "That's my girl." He nodded toward Davidenko. "So when do I die?"

"That is the question, isn't it?" Novak reasoned and drank some of the vodka. "You won't be so easy to kill. The fact that you're a government operative is less complicated than dealing with your family. We both know they won't rest until they discover the truth behind your disappearance." Novak paused, considering. Glass in hand, he returned to his seat at the poker table. "I'd have to call in a lot of favors."

"Favors from Davidenko's government friends?" Ian stretched his fingers until he felt the seam of his pocket. "The ones in Davidenko's computer? I have a copy of those files and I can guarantee in less than twenty-four hours, your friends won't be available. They'll be dealing with my friends."

"I underestimated you, MacAlister." Novak stopped, his gaze lethal. "And your girlfriend." He leaned back, placed an ankle on his knee and studied

Ian. "For your sake I hope she shows up with the *Katts Smeart* antidote."

"Don't you mean the formula and the antidote?"

"No, just the antidote," Novak said, his mouth twisted maliciously.

Ian understood then. "It was never about the formula, was it?"

"No. Only the antidote."

Ian strained against the cuffs, ignoring the bite of steel against his wrists, the trickle of blood across his palms. "Once there is an epidemic, people will need to be inoculated. The person with the antidote will stand to make a lot of money."

"Not only money," Novak agreed. "But that person will be hailed a hero. After all, how many people have saved the world?"

"And only a few thousand lives will be forfeited," Ian murmured. The tips of his finger touched the seam of his back pocket. Bit by bit, Ian drew out a short, thin wire.

"Sacrifices, remember?"

"And wiping out the Russian Mafia leaders? Was that part of the plan or just a bonus?" Ian worked the wire into the handcuff lock.

"Oh, that was the plan. Your money wasn't the only contaminated money. Davidenko's bills were just as deadly.

"The money you took from the desert was meant to be dispersed by the government banks. We both know that eventually the government ends up pocketing confiscated money. It would've taken a few months, of course. Considering how slow the government moves on anything. But eventually, we would have had another epidemic on our hands."

"Confirming your hero status?" Lara spoke from the doorway. Her gaze slid to Alexei, who stood, gun raised.

Ian took in her bloody arm, the bruises along her cheek and chin. A cold fury whipped through him.

"A little late for guns, don't you think?" Lara commented with disdain. "No one's at the elevator to protect you, Novak. Very sloppy."

Cain? Ian disregarded the notion. Cain and his men wouldn't have taken out the security yet. He wasn't to move in until Ian gave the signal. Too much was at stake.

Novak took in the ripped jeans, dirty T-shirt. "Maybe you scared him away." He glanced over his shoulder. "Alexei."

The bodyguard crossed the room and patted Lara down for weapons. "She's clean." He tossed her purse to Novak.

"Miss Mercer, your boyfriend and I were making small talk while waiting for you." Novak nodded toward Lara's mini backpack. "Your half an hour was almost over."

Alexei dumped the contents of her purse onto the table.

"Traffic." Her eyes touched briefly on Ian. Noted the split lip, reddened cheek in a glance. She saw one shoulder flex, the slight movement of his mouth. *Stall.*

Novak picked up the worn, leather Bible. "My father's. May I ask why you have it?"

"A memento," she commented, taking in her options. Alexei held a weapon, but Novak stood closer. "I collect them now and again."

"Well, you won't mind if I keep this one, then?" Novak tossed it onto the briefcase.

"You switched cases on me in the trailer the other night." Choosing Novak, Lara stepped toward the table. "That's why you attacked me after I picked up the briefcase. You had to be sure the explosion wouldn't destroy it."

"That's right. Once you escaped with the money, you were supposed to follow me here. I had planned on killing you then."

"Except you never got a good look at me."

"No, but a teenager did. The one you ran into after Sophia died," Novak sighed, shoving the purse away.

Lara risked another glance at Ian. *Soon.*

"This is tedious. We are here to negotiate for the antidote—"

"And Sophia?" Lara asked, hoping to touch a sensitive chord. "She wasn't supposed to die, was she?"

Novak froze, his eyes narrowed. "She was an unforeseen casualty."

"A casualty? And your baby's death? What was

that?" Lara asked, prodding his emotions. "It was your baby Sophia miscarried, wasn't it?"

"You are clever," Novak said, but his smile didn't quite thaw the blue ice of his gaze.

"No, not clever. Sophia's last words were, 'I gave it to father…my baby…mistake.' At the time I'd thought she meant Father Xavier—and that her baby had been a mistake. It was only later, when I realized she'd given you—the father of her baby—the agent and in doing so, made a mistake."

"Davidenko was too greedy to want children." Novak waved his hand. "One morning he discovered her throwing up and figured it out."

"I didn't realize… Not even when she gave me the *Katts Smeart.* But she told my father. She'd grown fond of him after I introduced them. He'd become her surrogate father, her confessor."

"Angry, irrational over the death of your baby, she decided to go after the *Katts Smeart,*" Lara surmised. A natural reaction, considering.

"For revenge." Novak ground out the words. "I taught her how to pickpocket. She became quite good in a small amount of time. But instead of giving me the combination to Davidenko's safe, she stole the files herself."

"When Davidenko discovered the chemical agent and its files gone," Lara guessed, "he immediately zeroed in on Sophia."

"She'd left too many clues," Novak said. "She'd

changed, she couldn't hide her disdain from Davidenko anymore. She jeopardized her safety. And the operation."

"So you cut her loose when Davidenko grew suspicious." Lara nodded, understanding. "Is that how your father gained possession of the antidote equations?"

"Sophia gave me the *Katts Smeart* agent, and my father the antidote information, just in case one of us was discovered."

Relief cascaded through Lara. If Novak had the agent, chances were slight that his father had poisoned the cross. "But you never got the antidote."

"At first my father held on to it, agreeing with Sophia. Then I became contaminated from the briefcase. I didn't tell my father until after the arms deal in the desert."

"By then, Davidenko had discovered Sophia's betrayal and his suspicions were aroused. It took longer than you expected to meet with your father."

"When we did, I told him of Sophia's death," Novak said. "Told him how she put the operation at risk. I thought my father understood. I should've known—" Novak sneered. "He hid the formula for the antidote in the hotel room—the one he got for your meeting, knowing you wouldn't have searched there. He insisted on waiting for you in the room—telling me you'd show up there sooner or later for the antidote."

"But I don't need it, do I?" Lara asked quietly. "You never contaminated his rosary. In the Catholic faith, when the priest blesses an object, it's treated with reverence. Father Xavier wouldn't have used the rosary for murder."

"Of course, there was the chance you'd touch the money," Novak speculated. "But my father insisted we needed only to convince you of the poisoning. Your involvement and subsequent death was the main object," Novak commented. "After I killed you, my father planned on killing himself. It would've appeared as a murder-suicide."

"Because of his cancer, taking the fall had been an easy decision." Lara caught Ian's eye. A slow blink told her he was ready. She let her arms hang to her side, relaxed. "He'd be classified as a government agent gone rogue."

"Yes, yes. But he lied," Novak scorned. He got up to pace, his irritation showing in every step. "In the room he told me of the baby, then he called me a coward. He said a hero would've risked everything, including his life, to protect a mother and child. He told me he'd risked his own soul to save mine. Before I could convince him otherwise, he pulled the gun on me."

"So you killed him, searched the room and found nothing—assumed he'd lied again. Then you gave Joseph your father's keys and the security code to the church." Lara saw Ian glance at the knife in

Davidenko's chest. She braced herself. Alexei held a gun and Novak had to reach for one. Ian's target would be Alexei.

"Joseph saw you with the paparazzi and decided to follow you first. Turned out you were headed to the same place."

"The formula for the antidote wasn't at St. Stan's," Lara remarked. "It was in his room here, at the Bontecou."

"You lie," Novak spat. "I searched the room."

"But you didn't know what you were looking for. I did." She nodded toward the table, calculated the distance between her and the pistol. "His Bible. Turn to Matthew, chapter twenty-six. Start at verse one. Over the words, he wrote the biochemical and antidote equations in a fluorescent ink. Your bar has a black light. I checked."

"What?" Novak grabbed the Bible.

Viktor rushed through the doorway. "Mr. Novak, government agents are swarming—"

Ian crashed to the floor, grasped the knife in Davidenko's chest. "Down, Lara!" Ian threw the blade.

Alexei dropped his gun and clawed at the knife now imbedded in his throat.

Novak grabbed for the gun on the table, just as Viktor swung his level with Ian.

No time! her mind screamed. Lara dived into Ian and the two guns exploded.

Ian grunted, jerked back, his arms automatically

locked around Lara. His back hit the floor, taking the impact of the fall.

"She just saved your life, MacAlister," Novak shouted. He grabbed the briefcase and followed Viktor out the door.

"Of all the stupid—" Ian stopped, registered the sticky warmth seeping between his fingers. Terror, stark and vivid, slammed into him. "Lara?"

"Two guns, no choice," she rasped, her head lolled against his shoulder. "Go. Stop Novak."

"Lara!" Ian's hand cupped her cheek, saw her eyes flutter. "Stay with me."

"Stop him!" Her lips, paled from the pain, barely moved. "He took Armand's briefcase. Too many people will die."

"So will you, if I don't—"

"No." Lara shuddered against him and anguish squeezed his chest, blocked his throat. He knew what she was asking, he just wasn't sure if he had the courage to obey. "Please."

Ian swore. "Don't you dare die on me, Red," he whispered, his voice ragged with raw, primitive grief. Gently, he lowered her to the floor, brushed her hair from her face. "I swear to God, after this we're done. Do you hear me? No more."

"Yes. No more." Tears trembled on her lashes before dropping to her chalky white cheeks. "Go!"

Ian's lips brushed hers. He tasted the dampness, knew its salty flavor would stay with him forever.

Then without looking back, he snagged Alexei's gun and took off running.

IAN TOOK THE ROOF STAIRS two at a time and burst out the door. Gunfire exploded around him. He froze, but didn't take cover. Instead he studied the sleek, white helicopter as it fired up—the propellers whipping up dust and grit from its roof pad.

"MacAlister! Get rid of the gun!" Novak's voice boomed from the speaker. "Or I open this case over the streets of Vegas."

Ian dropped his weapon, then kicked it away. With deliberate movements, he locked his fingers behind his head. Two men lay unmoving on the edge of the helicopter pad. Both were dressed in white anticontamination suits—now stained with their blood. Viktor's work, no doubt.

"You've lost," Ian shouted. He stepped a few feet toward Novak, gauging the distance. The wind was strong, but that couldn't be helped. He nodded toward the dead bodies. "The calvary is here."

"I have the Bible. If your friends want to negotiate, they better be ready to save me when I contact them. Otherwise, the antidote dies with me." Novak twirled his hand, signaling Viktor to lift off.

Ian found the face of his watch under his index finger. The helicopter rose off the pad. He counted. Five, ten, fifteen feet.

"Then I guess it dies with you," he murmured and

twisted the watch face. A split second later, the helicopter burst into flames.

THE EXPLOSION ROCKED the roof beneath Ian's feet. But it was the fire that concerned him. Bits of steel and glass showered the roof.

"What the bloody hell?" Jordan Beck came running out of the stairway door. Long, lanky strides closing the distance between the two men.

"Beck, make sure there's no money debris. I planted Kate's minibomb in the briefcase lock. The explosion should have incinerated any paper inside the case but we can't take a chance," Ian yelled and started down the stairs. He hit the boardroom on a dead run.

And slammed into a human wall.

"Damn it, Quamar," Ian yelled. He looked past the giant, saw blood on the floor, but no Lara.

He grabbed his friend's shirt in his fists. It didn't matter that Quamar Bazan stood a good half foot taller than Ian. Or that the bald-headed giant had fifty pounds on him.

He'd take on hell itself if he had to. "Where is she?"

"On her way to the hospital." Quamar's words were low, his accent heavy but soothing. His leather-brown eyes softened with concern.

Neither helped ease Ian's fears, but he let go of Quamar's shirt. "Was she conscious?"

"Yes." Quamar inclined his head.

"She knew I called in the troops then."

"She saw both Beck and myself."

"I need to go. She might…the baby…" Ian stepped away. "Which hospital?"

Quamar grabbed his arm, held him. "It does not matter, Ian, we are quarantined. Lara, too. Two hundred men in white plastic suits guard the hotel. All are armed with stun guns."

Ian remembered the dead men on the roof. But it didn't matter. He'd no intention of staying.

Quamar frowned, guessing Ian's thoughts. "Even if you broke through their barriers, you would still have to deal with others that Cain has posted in the hospital."

"If you've got a point, Quamar. Make it."

"You are being selfish, my friend. The fact that it is motivated by love and concern does not make it any less selfish. You want to risk exposing her and the baby, so you can clear your conscience and tell her you love her," Quamar reasoned. "She already knows."

"Quamar's right, Yank." Jordan walked into the room. Sympathy reduced the Englishman's sharp features. He and Quamar had both lost family. They understood. "Lara has enough to deal with right now." He placed a hand on his friend's shoulder and squeezed. "Cain's with her. And so is Jon Mercer. And your parents are on their way." Jordan grinned at Ian's scowl. "Your mother saw the news report."

Ian nodded. He knew his mother well enough, that Christel would be by Lara's side within the hour.

"Cain gave his word," Jordan continued, handing

Ian a cell phone, "that he would call every fifteen minutes with updates. She'll have the best of care and you'll be the first to know."

Ian saw bloodstains spattered on Quamar's shirt and pants. Lara's blood. "You held her, before help came."

"Yes."

A red haze filled his peripheral vision. "Damn it, it should've been me." But he'd been busy saving the world. "Did she say anything…?"

"Yes," Quamar murmured. "She said Novak had the wrong Bible."

Chapter Sixteen

Five months later…

I SWEAR TO GOD, *after this, we're done. Do you hear me?*

No more.

Lara's gazed drifted over the splashes of gold, the strokes of emerald that covered the autumn hills, the sapphire of the lake in between. Soft, serene. A soothing balance to the dusk's velvet hues of indigo and pink that flared just beyond.

The breeze drifted across the lace curtains, dusting them back from the wide, French doors. On the soft current of air, came the sweet scent of roses, cypress and elm from her mother's gardens.

Lara had lived the last four months in her mother's château, seventy-five kilometers from Paris. During that time, she'd walked the gardens—sometimes alone, most times with her mama—listening to the chatter of the squirrels and the more mournful cry of the quail. Letting the peacefulness of the French countryside quiet away her doubts, soothe the aches in her heart.

Through it all, she'd never been free of Ian's final words. *I'm done. No more.*

Lara tipped her forehead, resting it against the bay window, enjoying the cool glass against her skin. It had been five months since Ian had said those words, five months since she'd woken up in the hospital, drained of strength and worse, hope—not sure if her baby had survived her surgery.

A surgery that had cost her a lot of blood and some of her lower intestines.

But they'd both pulled through.

Her hand drifted over her extended stomach. Somewhere beneath the gauzy cotton of her dress, lay the scar. Meaningless now, considering.

She'd spent a month in the hospital, two weeks of it quarantined. During that time, Ian's family had visited her every waking moment of every day. Sharing stories, mostly of Ian, some of their family history, even parts of their own lives with her.

Her dad, too. Emotion squeezed at Lara's throat over the memory. Jon Mercer had been the first person she'd seen after regaining consciousness—his gloved hand the first thing she felt as it clasped hers.

Later, he'd said that almost losing her was his greatest gift. A father-daughter relationship.

While quarantined, she'd found out many things

she'd never known. His years of loneliness and anger over what he'd given up. His fear when Lara had decided to follow his path in life.

How he still loved her mother.

Hours on hours, he talked of her mother. How each day, Lara grew in her image.

The ache of what she'd missed had grown over that month. By the time she'd been discharged, Lara understood she couldn't go forward without the last piece of the puzzle. Meeting her mother.

A muscle spasm jarred her lower back. More than a little awkward, Lara pushed out her belly and shifted positions. Realizing immediately that she'd succeeded only in putting pressure on her bladder, she smiled and tried another position.

Lara loved being pregnant—backaches and all.

Now, at seven months, she'd long ago shed her fears of motherhood and embraced the direction her life would take.

Lara leaned back against the wall and rested her hand across her swollen belly. She cherished this time alone with her thoughts, with her baby. She closed her eyes, allowing the last burst of sunlight to heat her cheeks, her thoughts to drift.

During her stay in the hospitals, Ian hadn't come to see her. Whenever she'd mention him to his family, they'd evade or change the subject. Finally understanding her question caused them pain, Lara stopped asking.

The baby rolled, causing her belly to wave mid-breath. She rubbed it softly—murmured loving, soothing promises.

"Are you all right, *ma petite?*"

Lara looked up from the window seat. Shantelle Laroche stood in the doorway of the sitting room. In the soft light of evening, most would take in the soft, delicate features, the mahogany hair and place Shantelle barely passed the age of forty.

At fifty-five, she'd kept her figure trim, from long walks and a small appetite. And, Lara suspected, a long line of attentive lovers.

It wasn't a fussing comment, but one of concern. "I'm fine, Mama." Her mother didn't fuss. "Your grandchild is restless."

"Maybe my grandbaby knows she will meet her papa today."

Lara's head shot up, her eyes narrowed. "What are you talking about?"

Her mother tsked, pleased. "Just the mention of him puts color in your cheeks. That's the way love should be." Shantelle's lips curved. "I came in to tell you, you have a visitor. A handsome visitor." A delicate eyebrow arched. "My future son-in-law maybe, yes?"

"Nothing maybe about it," came the impatient masculine reply.

Ian strolled into the room, his laser-blue eyes pinned Lara to her seat, daring her to move.

"Madam, I believe your maid has fainted. It seems my unwillingness to stay in the parlor frightened her."

"Ian?"

Shantelle's smile increased over her daughter's confusion. Unable to resist, she grabbed Ian's hand and squeezed, drawing his attention. "It's Maria's temperament, not your fierceness, I'm sorry to say. The poor girl faints every time she sees a spider. I must go make sure she is fine." Shantelle started to leave, then turned back. "There is a lock on the door, Monsieur MacAlister. May I suggest you use it?"

"Mama!"

Shantelle took a long, lingering glance at her daughter. They'd had only a few months together, such a short moment. But now, it was time to share her. "Yes, I am your mama. But I am still French. And so is your temper, *ma petite.*"

"Thank you, madam," Ian said with a slow sexy wink.

Shantelle's breath caught. Oh yes, she would have fine grandchildren. And many, too.

Happiness filled her. Shantelle planned on being a better *grandmère* than a mother. Although, she thought, slipping out of the room, her maternal instincts had definitely improved in the last few months.

Ian closed the door, snapped the lock in place.

"Really, Ian, I'm seven months pregnant. If I run anywhere, it's going to be to the bathroom."

"That's not the reason I locked the door," he

said quietly, his eyes drinking her features from across the room.

Clumsily, Lara stood. Sunbeams shot through the thin gossamer sundress, outlining her supple, rounded body underneath. Her hair was down, longer now. Her features softer with pregnancy pounds.

An ache squeezed the breath from his chest. "I should have done this the first time I met you," he stated, his voice hoarse with emotion.

"What? Locked me in a room?"

"No. Gotten you pregnant."

He heard her breath catch, and love shimmered under his heart.

Slowly, Ian crossed to her, stopping mere inches from the window seat. He fisted his hands, not ready to touch her. Knowing if he did, the explanations wouldn't come until much later. Explanations that needed to be made now.

"I think once we work out our differences and get married, I'm going to keep you pregnant." His gaze caressed her form, pausing slightly on her stomach, before continuing down to her uncovered feet.

The blue of his eyes flared. "And barefooted."

Lara's toes curled into the Persian rug.

"If you're trying to win me with your Neanderthal ideas, it isn't working," she taunted, more than a little breathless. He could see it in her eyes, the flash of awareness, the same longing he'd suffered through for the last several months.

"Liar." He drew the word out, in a long, soft caress.

Lara shivered, and it took every bit of willpower he had not to reach for her.

"I've already won you, Red," Ian murmured. "You've already admitted you love me."

"I can love you and still not like you."

Ian smirked, but continued as if she hadn't spoken. "If you're nice, after we're married, I'll let you help me run MacAlister Whiskey—although I don't think it will be enough. Whether we like it or not, you're high energy, Red." Ian saw her mouth tremble. "We're definitely going to need a lot of children to keep you busy. And maybe a dog or two."

She tried to step back, stopped when her knees hit the window seat. "Not funny—"

"Did I tell you, we're going to grow old together?" He moved closer, stalking her. "Watch our grandchildren play? Hold each other's hands while taking in a sunset or two?"

Lara would have taken a deep breath, worked the knot from her chest, if only he hadn't locked gazes.

His features had roughened, the lines of his face had sharpened, his mouth hardened. A few days of whiskers did nothing to soften the harsh angles. But his eyes did. Glittering in the blue depths was a promise of something. She wasn't sure what, but it got her pulse pounding, her heart wishing she believed in fairy tales.

"Stop it, Ian." She put her hand to his chest, out of self-preservation. He was seducing her with dreams. And damn it, it was working.

"You lied to me. First about my father. Then when you called in Cain and Jordan." The fact Lara had understood and gotten over it, didn't stop her from throwing the accusation out there. If he wasn't going to give her a chance, she was going to fight dirty going down. "And Quamar."

"You ran from me. We're even." He trailed a finger over her hand, down to the hollow of her elbow, paused, then retraced his path.

"I didn't run," Lara argued, tried not to close her eyes, lose herself in his touch. "People knew where I was."

"My whole family it seemed. My sister especially. She and Roman have decided we're going to be godparents for their baby girl. Already, little Kyla is showing signs of being a daredevil."

She grasped his wrist to stop the movement of his fingers. "She's only a few weeks old."

"Doesn't matter. We Scots know these things," he said with arrogance. "Kate says that Kyla is going to need a butt-kicking godmother to keep her out of trouble."

A godmother. Before she could stop it, the tears burned her throat. "Kate and I have become close—the whole pregnancy thing. I needed advice," Lara whispered huskily. Then her chin shot out, Irish stubborn. "I love your family, Ian, and I won't apologize for it."

"They love you, too. And I don't expect an apology. Maybe a really nice thank-you—later." Ian tugged his hand free, then touched his finger to her lips, traced the curve until it quivered. "But remember you loved me first."

"Conceited," she retorted, but with no power behind her words. Instead, she nipped the end of his finger. Watched his eyes flare with awareness.

"Why did you leave me, Lara?" He cupped the curve of her cheek, but his gaze remained on her mouth.

"I had no choice." Her tongue slipped out, moistened her lips. "Everything happened so fast."

Ian saw her tongue, trembled with need. "But it was over. I'd gotten the whole thing on camera. Novak admitting his guilt. The poker game. All of it recorded through my tie clip. After we retrieved the right Bible from Father Xavier's hotel room, I handed it all over to Cain."

She closed her eyes, lost herself in the touch of his palm. The calloused skin sent goose bumps running down the base of her neck. "I needed to figure out who I was. It's trite, but it was true. I couldn't do that with you around. You, you—" Confuse me, she wanted to say. Instead, she said, "You told me no more. You were done."

"I was. No more Labyrinth. No more operations. No more lies."

"You lied," she said, jerking her head up, unable to keep the hurt from her words. "I understand you were doing your duty, Ian, but we were partners—"

"No, Lara, being partners is a business arrangement," he corrected. "When I brought Cain in, it wasn't business, it was personal. You were in danger."

"I see." But she didn't. She'd decided long ago to forgive him because he'd made the call, done his duty. Now the resentment poured back in, opening old wounds.

"I wasn't going to lose you. Bottom line. I had to do whatever it took to keep you safe."

"Me?" She wrenched away, angry with herself, angrier with him. "You risked all those people's lives to save mine? Do you realize what could've happened?"

"Do you realize what did happen?" Ian responded, then snatched her back. "I walked away from you, and almost lost you and the baby because of it." Ian took a deep shuddered breath, tipped his forehead to hers. "I've spent most of my life saving people. I've seen enough violence, enough death to last a hundred lifetimes. I've taken it all on the chin and gone back for more. Why? Because of duty. But in that moment, with you on the floor, me helpless to save you, my heart stopped. I've relived the picture of you, bloody, pale—dying—a million times."

"You stopped Novak. You did what you had to do."

"I didn't care about Novak, don't you see?" Ian

pulled back until his eyes found hers. "If you know anything about me, sweetheart, you have to know family is everything to me. And you're my family. You always have been. Since the first moment I saw you across that dance floor. I just didn't put the feelings into thoughts until recently." He tipped her chin up, caught a stray tear with his thumb. "Why do you think I resigned from the Navy to join Labyrinth? I didn't need to prove anything. With Kate and Cain, I wanted to be there," Ian explained. "When you joined, I *had* to be there."

"How about before? When my father almost died?"

"When you grieved, it ripped a mile-wide hole in my chest. But even then, I wouldn't change what I did," he pointed out. "Remember over a year ago, when Roman and Kate were on the run from that sadistic arms dealer? He almost killed them. Cain and I thought we'd lost them. But even then, even the possibility of losing Kate, didn't compare to almost losing you—" Ian took a deep breath. "I knew what you were going through. You were angry, out of your mind with grief and revenge. Do you think that would've changed, knowing Jon wasn't dead? You would've still gone after the killer. I couldn't let you."

He was right. Like Sophia, Lara had only one thought. To strike back.

"If something had happened to you…" Ian stopped, his jaw flexed.

"Promise me, Ian. That you'll never lie to me again. Even if I won't like the truth."

"I already promised you, Red. When I left you in that room, gut shot and bleeding to death. You. Not you and the baby. Just you," he said.

"Are you saying, you don't care—"

"I love our baby, but my world is you," he interrupted. "It will always be you. That's why I let you make the call that day. And why I went after Novak. If that isn't love I don't know what is."

"Ian, I'm sorry." She shook her head, not knowing what else to say. Not knowing if she would have been strong enough to do the same—leave him lying on the floor dying.

"Good. Then it won't happen again, right?"

A smile curved her lips. "If you hadn't heard, I quit Labyrinth."

"I heard. But somehow, trouble gravitates toward you," Ian observed. His hands slid over the round curve of her butt, before continuing to the base of her spine. Slowly, he massaged the muscles beneath. "That's why I quit, too. If nothing else, just to keep an eye on you."

Lara sank into him with a sigh. "You quit?"

"Three months ago."

"I don't understand—"

"I told you, I'm taking over the whiskey side of MacAlister Industries. With Cain being Labyrinth's director and Kate and Roman no longer active,

I was the only one left of the family doing field-work."

"But Cain—"

"It will be fine. Labyrinth's got new blood coming in."

"No more operations? No more bad guys?"

"Scared?" Ian teased. "A normal life can be pretty intimidating. But if the whiskey business doesn't thrill you, Red, you can think about becoming an instructor. Lord knows, Cain's going to need them."

"What about Celeste?"

Ian grinned. "We're guessing twins. They just found out and Cain is beside himself. It's almost unnatural. One moment he's grinning like a lunatic, the next he's frowning because he thinks Celeste is too small to carry two babies." Ian gave an exaggerated shiver. "He's spooking Celeste. She says you'd better come home soon, because she needs lots of advice from you and Kate."

"Twins?" Lara slid her hands over his chest, slipped the tips of her fingers into the V-neck of his sweater, needing the contact of his skin against hers. "Do they run in your family?"

"Looks like it." Ian's hand found hers, held it in place. "Why? Do you want a set of your own?" he murmured.

"Maybe," she whispered. "I love being pregnant, Ian, but I can't wait to meet our baby."

Ian nuzzled her temple, then kissed it. "Me, neither."

"Funny, I never thought Celeste would give up profiling."

"She's not." Ian slid onto the window seat, brought Lara down into his lap. "She'll have plenty of help. That's the beauty of family. You really don't have to give up anything."

"Really?"

"Except privacy." Ian's brows knitted into a frown. "Even long distance, a day hasn't gone by that I haven't gotten advice from my parents or Cain or Kate or your father."

"My father?"

"Believe it or not, he's the worst," Ian announced. "Once we're home, you're answering all the phone calls to the house."

Home. It sounded so wonderful. "Ian, how come you took so long? To come here I mean. I didn't really hide where I was going. And with your skill for—"

"Hunting?" Ian shifted Lara until she faced him, straddling his hips, her belly settled comfortably against his hard stomach.

"Sweetheart, I haven't been anywhere else. I was on your Air France flight out here." One hand supported her back, while the other trailed up over her knee, catching the hem of her dress. "I just made sure you didn't see me."

Ian laughed at her stunned expression. "I promised your dad, I'd give you time." Later Ian would tell her of the three-hour lecture, the threats. And after, how he agreed to leave Lara alone in order to get Jon Mercer's blessing.

"I took a summerhouse, not far from here." His fingers skimmed the line of her knee, the warm curve of her thigh, catching the cotton and nudging it aside to stroke the sensitive underside of her leg.

Lara's limbs tightened reflexively against his, causing him to swell uncomfortably against his zipper. "You've been following me?"

Impatient to finish, to feel her legs around him, her body naked against him, Ian confessed. "Hell yes. Waiting until you were ready. Then yesterday in the garden, I saw you laughing. The baby must have moved because you held your stomach. And I knew it was time."

She nodded, remembering. "He did move."

"He?"

"I think so, but Mama insists it's a girl. But he's so active." Ian's hand slid under her dress, over her belly. "I was all wrong about Mama. She'd made the wrong choices, let her family dictate her life. After she was forced to give me up, she eventually walked away from them all." Lara plucked at his shirt, embarrassed by her own shortsightedness. "She's wonderful, Ian. Intelligent, strong."

"No surprise there. You're her daughter." Ian trailed his lips across her cheek, tasted the corner of her mouth. "I also happen to agree with her about the baby."

Lara gave his hair a sharp tug and he chuckled. "Don't get me wrong, I want boys, too. Lots of them. But a little girl like you would be the perfect—"

"Butt kicker?"

Ian kissed her nose. "No, the perfect miracle."

Lara found Ian's hand beneath her dress and moved it over to her side.

When the baby bumped his palm, the muscle in his jaw flexed. "God, you're amazing."

"Thanks," she murmured, more than willing to take the credit for the moment.

"So what about it?" he asked, his voice soaked with emotion. "Are you ready to come home, Red?"

"No."

When his eyes snapped to hers, she let the humor show through. "Not until you tell me the reason."

"I love you. And if that's not reason enough," Ian said, "I watched you get shot, I spent a month of quarantine with Quamar and Jordan—which was no picnic. Do you realize the more bored and short-tempered they got, the heavier their accents became? They gave me a headache."

"Quamar?" Lara loved Quamar, had seen him only a week past. The giant stopped by to check on her before heading home to the desert and to his people. "He's never short-tempered." But there was a sadness lurking behind the soft brown of his eyes. When she'd questioned him, he hugged her.

Told her to trust her instincts, trust Ian. And they would be happy.

But Quamar never answered her question.

"Believe me, Quamar is not easy to deal with when he's been cooped up behind walls," Ian retorted. "Then I spent another four months listening to your father's advice on marriage."

Ian let out a long exaggerated sigh. "I know you love him, honey, but—"

"Marriage? I thought he was giving you advice on children."

"No, I figure that advice will come after the baby and won't stop until we're done with our first half dozen."

"A half dozen?" Lara gasped.

"Maybe more." Ian winked. "Right now he's trying to work up the nerve to ask your mother to marry him. Somehow I think he's channeling that fear by telling me how to be a good husband."

"My parents are getting married?"

"Stay focused, Red," Ian complained. "I love you. Come home with me."

"I am home. We both are. You're our home, Ian." Lara smoothed her hand over the baby. "But you haven't answered my question."

"What question?" Ian murmured, his mouth traveling down the side of her neck.

She tipped her head back, allowing him more access. "Why you felt the need to lock the door."

"The door?"

"Yes, I distinctly remember saying..." He nipped at the delicate hollow of her collarbone, then immediately soothed the spot with his tongue.

Lara trembled. "I wasn't running anywhere. But you locked me in anyway."

"I didn't explain?" Ian's mouth dipped between her breasts, kissed the rapid beat of her heart, watched her nipples pucker in response. "I thought for sure..."

"Ian..." His mouth found her beaded nub, nibbled at it through the cotton. Lara gasped, and her insides liquefied.

"It's my hormones, Red." Ian returned to her mouth, nudged her lips apart. "They're raging."

Epilogue

Quentin "Mac" MacAlister watched the young couple twirl around the dance floor from his place beside the bar. The bride's pearl-white evening gown sparkled in the ballroom lights with a radiance that only a new love merited.

They'd been married several weeks already, having done the deed in France. Mac's disappointment at not seeing his final child wed was forgotten when the couple circled in front of him. Lara MacAlister's face beamed. She blew her father-in-law a kiss and showed off her belly—big with child.

"They're beautiful together, aren't they, Mac?"

Without looking away from the sight, he hugged his own bride of forty years. "That they are, Christel. That they are."

She sighed the sigh of a mother losing her last child. One of joy, but forlorn at the same time. Mac turned toward her and smiled with affection. Not quite a foot shorter than his own six-two, with sea-smoked eyes and hair the color of ravens, Christel MacAlister was blessed with the refined features of her Scottish ancestors. The same features which left her with the beauty of a woman in her forties rather than her sixties.

She smiled back, love shimmering in her eyes.

"He's good for her, dearest. He chased away her fears," Mac said. Fears that couldn't be hidden from family, he thought.

"She chased away his, too."

"Aye, she did." Mac chuckled. Leave it to his lass to balance the scales. A trait she had passed on to their daughter Kate and now to their daughters-in-law, Celeste and Lara.

"They'll have a strong child. With Scot blood running through him," he said with an arrogance that survived a dozen generations. His gaze shifted once again back to the center of the floor where the music had stopped and an impromptu applause was taking place. He watched Ian pull Lara into his arms and kiss her with a fierceness that roused some cheering.

To think he'd almost lost them both six months ago. Fear prodded his heart, but Mac quickly banished the feeling. It was the time for celebrating life and its blessings, not worrying about what might have been.

He could already see a titian-haired baby on his lap, smiling and cooing, tugging on his thick white beard. The picture restored his good humor and he toasted the couple with the glass of whiskey in his hand. "Yes, fine Scottish babies."

"Who'll be half Irish, MacAlister. The better half I'm thinking."

A hefty slap on Mac's shoulder sent the liquor spewing from his mouth.

He swung around to see Jon Mercer grinning with delight. The man falls in love, and somehow finds a sense of humor after thirty years. A funny sight on a bulldog face, thought Mac perversely as he wiped his chin. "You just wasted forty-year-old scotch, man. That's a sin against God."

Mac sighed. The man was family now. Although Mac hadn't decided if he'd vote for Mercer if he decided to run for President. They'd yet to debate any issues. Then there was the fact, Mercer was ex-army. Anyone with half a brain knew the Navy was the only military worth serving.

"Don't forget our grandchild will be carrying the name Mercer." Jon smiled, not the least bit intimated by Mac's scowl.

A promise his boy, Ian, had made. And if it was a girl? Mac thought. What kind of name would that be for an angel? "I won't be forgetting that, you Irish—"

"Quentin MacAlister."

Mac bit off the last word while the bulldog laughed. In his lifetime, he'd gone head-to-head with many world leaders, often taking pleasure in the fight. Christel was another matter. Experience had taught him when his wife used a certain tone of voice, it never paid to tangle with her because he never won. He adored the woman, but sometimes she could be a tyrant and Ian's reception wasn't the time or the place to do battle. Not if he wanted to live.

Mac suspected Mercer knew it, too, if the glint in the man's eye was any indication.

After a stern look at her husband, Christel smiled at their guest. "Would you care for a drink, Jon? Mac has brought a bottle of his best for the occasion. I'm sure he would like you to join him in a toast." The elbow that jabbed Mac's stomach wasn't as gracious as her next question. "Wouldn't you, Mac?"

Mac sighed rather than cringed at the words, his bushy white brows drawing together into a deep V while he poured the drink for Mercer. One more waste of his best scotch. Irish, hah! The thought of conspiring with the enemy grated against every bone that made him a MacAlister. Nevertheless, he'd do it to keep the peace at Ian's reception. With a last glance at his wife's determined expression, Mac raised his glass with the bulldog's.

"Here's to the baby's *last* name. A Scottish dynasty in the making," Jon proposed.

"I'll not be drinking to any toast you'd—"

Startled, Mac stopped and looked at the Irishman, whose expression was full of amusement. "A dynasty?" Mac stroked his beard.

Kate's husband, Roman, was Italian. They'd given Mac a beautiful cherub, Kyla Anne MacAlister, with raven hair like her grandma and Mac's own blue eyes.

And now Cain's wife, Celeste, was expecting in the spring. With twins.

It *was* a good beginning.

"Well now, a dynasty. There's a thought." He studied Mercer, suddenly pleased. The heathen might not be so bad after all. And Mac certainly wasn't the type of fellow to hold a grudge. What's more, Christel liked the sod and Mac enjoyed indulging his wife whenever possible.

Suddenly, Ian picked up Lara and twirled her around. Laughter rang out from the dance floor. Mac's mouth curved slightly. *Aye, the boy will cherish the lass.*

Mac slapped his friend on the back and grinned when the whiskey sloshed a bit. "A toast then," he said, his agreement booming across the room like a cannon. "To the last name, MacAlister."

* * * * *

Happily ever after is just the beginning…

Turn the page for a sneak preview of
DANCING ON SUNDAY AFTERNOONS
by
Linda Cardillo

Prologue

Giulia D'Orazio
1983

I had two husbands—Paolo and Salvatore.

Salvatore and I were married for thirty-two years. I still live in the house he bought for us; I still sleep in our bed. All around me are the signs of our life together. My bedroom window looks out over the garden he planted. In the middle of the city, he coaxed tomatoes, peppers, zucchini—even grapes for his wine—out of the ground. On weekends, he used to drive up to his cousin's farm in Waterbury and bring back manure. In the winter, he wrapped the peach tree and the fig tree with rags and black rubber hoses against the cold, his massive, coarse hands gentling those trees as if they were his fragile-skinned babies. My neighbor, Dominic Grazza, does that for me now. My boys have no time for the garden.

In the front of the house, Salvatore planted roses. The roses I take care of myself. They are giant, cream-colored, fragrant. In the afternoons, I like to sit out on the porch with my coffee, protected from the eyes of the neighborhood by that curtain of flowers.

Salvatore died in this house thirty-five years ago. In the last months, he lay on the sofa in the parlor so he could be in the middle of everything. Except for the two oldest boys, all the children were still at home and we ate together every evening. Salvatore could see the dining room table from the sofa, and he could hear everything that was said. "I'm not dead, yet," he told me. "I want to know what's going on."

When my first grandchild, Cara, was born, we brought her to him and he held her on his chest, stroking her tiny head. Sometimes they fell asleep together.

Over on the radiator cover in the corner of the parlor is the portrait Salvatore and I had taken on our twenty-fifth anniversary. This brooch I'm wearing today, with the diamonds—I'm wearing it in the photograph also—Salvatore gave it to me that day. Upstairs on my dresser is a jewelry box filled with necklaces and bracelets and earrings. All from Salvatore.

I am surrounded by the things Salvatore gave me,

or did for me. But, God forgive me, as I lie alone now in my bed, it is Paolo I remember.

Paolo left me nothing. Nothing, that is, that my family, especially my sisters, thought had any value. No house. No diamonds. Not even a photograph.

But after he was gone, and I could catch my breath from the pain, I knew that I still had something. In the middle of the night, I sat alone and held them in my hands, reading the words over and over until I heard his voice in my head. I had Paolo's letters.

* * * * *

Silhouette
Desire

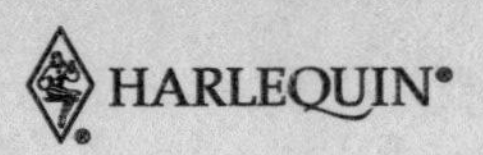

INTRIGUE®

COMING NEXT MONTH

#969 BIG SKY STANDOFF by B.J. Daniels

Montana Mystique

Stock detective Jacklyn Wilde needs Dillon Savage's help to corral a band of cowboys rustling cattle in the Montana prairie. What she doesn't need is his undeniable sex appeal messing up her investigation.

#970 SLEEPING BEAUTY SUSPECT by Dani Sinclair

It isn't every day that Flynn O'Shay gets to rescue a beautiful sleeping beauty from a fire and awaken her with a kiss. But a murderer lurks to ensure there is no storybook ending.

#971 TRACE EVIDENCE IN TARRANT COUNTY by Delores Fossen

The Silver Star of Texas

Texas Ranger Sloan McKinney returns to his hometown of Justice, Texas, to investigate two murders—one that's sixteen years cold and another that's red-hot—only to find himself working with his old nemesis, Sheriff Carley Matheson.

#972 COLD CASE COWBOY by Jenna Ryan

Detective Nick Law is certain that Sasha Myer fits into a killer's pattern. But to protect her he needs to reopen a long-dormant case—which will ignite Denver with passion and betrayal.

#973 SHADOW MOUNTAIN by Leona Karr

Starting a new life with her son, Caroline Fairchild accepts a job redecorating the mountain home of Texas maven Wes Wainwright. But someone is willing to tear her family apart and reveal everyone's past indiscretions.

#974 THE ENGLISH DETECTIVE AND THE ROOKIE AGENT by Pat White

The Blackwell Group

Investigator Jeremy Barnes relies more on intellect than instinct. In Mercedes Ramos he finds a partner who isn't shy about speaking her mind. But any difference of opinion will have to wait if they're to recover a missing boy and evade a brilliant mind stalking the Blackwell Group.